SECOND CHANCE

SECOND CHANCE

Terry Green

Matador
9 Priory Business Park,
Wistow Road, Kibworth Beauchamp,
Leicestershire. LE8 0RX
Tel: 0116 279 2299
Email: books@troubador.co.uk
Web: www.troubador.co.uk/matador
Twitter: @matadorbooks

ISBN 978 1800460 577

British Library Cataloguing in Publication Data.
A catalogue record for this book is available from the British Library.

Printed on FSC accredited paper
Printed and bound in Great Britain by 4edge Limited
Typeset in 11pt Minion Pro by Troubador Publishing Ltd, Leicester, UK

Matador is an imprint of Troubador Publishing Ltd

To Alison, my Second, Second Chance.

Prologue

It was fairly quiet in the Bull's Head on this particular evening. One family however, from outside the village, had decided to break their journey in order to obtain refreshments.

Joe Richards looked across from behind the bar to where the family had settled, and smiled. He had witnessed the scene so many times. Over in the far corner Josh Wilkins held his audience captive. What the family had no doubt planned was a quiet meal and drink at the Bull's Head, before going on their way. What they had not expected was entertainment in the shape of Josh Wilkins, village storyteller.

Josh had by this time worked his way through a number of local tales, and had been so far rewarded with a pint of best. Now he was working toward his favourite story.

"I take it you're keeping an eye on the lad missus," Josh said, as he took another sip of ale. He always liked that line, it was guaranteed to get their interest.

"What do you mean by that?" The woman asked, as she pulled her young son closer to her.

"He was about your lad's age."

"Who was?"

Josh emptied his glass, placed it down on the table, and smiled. There was a pause, and then the penny dropped.

"Another drink Josh?" Asked the boy's father.

"If you insist," the old rogue replied.

"And don't carry on until I get back, I want to hear the story as well."

"Don't worry mister, I'll wait." Josh looked across the room in the direction of Joe Richards, and smiled.

With a second pint safely in his hand, Josh resumed his tale.

"It were some years ago now mind, but yes he was about your lad's age. They never did find him, even when they emptied the canal. He just disappeared."

ONE

A New Face

There was nothing you could actually put your finger on, but there was certainly an atmosphere. You were either 'village' or 'newcomer'. Even those that had moved to Newton Magna twenty years previously were not considered 'village'. And there was the problem of house prices. The ability of some people, especially 'southerners', to purchase a second home in the country had pushed the prices sky high. Locals wishing to buy their first property just couldn't compete. As a consequence, the younger generation was being depleted, as many moved away from the area. The village was dying a slow death.

Newton Magna had always been a quiet village; it had no time for the hustle and bustle that came with modern life. It was proud to be part of the English countryside, and proud of its close connection with the land. The residents were more than pleased that The

Industrial Revolution had passed it by. Only the early canal engineers had deemed it worthy of attention. Even then, no working boats had loaded or unloaded there, they just passed steadily through. And if it hadn't have been necessary to build four locks to raise the level of the canal some twenty feet or so, it is doubtful if boaters would have given it a second glance. Even the great railway engineers, when they surveyed the land in the nineteenth century, chose nearby Market Clayton as the site for their goods yard. And that had now been reclaimed by nature, the rails having been lifted long ago. Only the ghosts of trains travelled along the old track bed these days. But the peace and quiet of the village of Newton Magna was being gradually eroded by two of its younger inhabitants, Jack Fletcher and Robert Bridges.

The Fletchers were newcomers to the village, having only moved there some eighteen months previously. Carol and Paul Fletcher had bought the house initially as an investment. But when Paul Fletcher's partners elected to relocate, there seemed little point in keeping the house in Essex. As a result, he bought a one bedroomed apartment for use during the week, and the family moved into 9 London Road as their principal home. Carol Fletcher was an unpublished author, and spent most of her time tapping away on her lap top. There were piles of unsubmitted manuscripts on the desk. She wanted to be a successful writer, but had never actually taken the final step. Her self – doubts prevented this.

When they had first met, Carol had admired Paul's commitment to work. He had a passion for success that would see him, and any future family well provided for. That passion had now become all consuming, and anything that was not work related took a poor second place. Jack missed his old friends, and by way of some compensation, would have liked to have spent more time with his dad. But Paul Fletcher was always 'too busy', and Jack was therefore more or less left to his own devices; little attention being paid to his activities. Paul Fletcher thought that it was only a matter of buying Jack something, and all would be well. Money was certainly not a problem, but his generosity often caused friction between Jack's parents. Carol Fletcher tried her best, but was finding the going difficult. Only that morning she had spoken with her son about values.

"That's the trouble with you, you think you're hard done by. What you don't realize is just how lucky you are. Years ago, people worked hard to survive, and had little or no luxuries. You get everything so easily," she had said.

Jack, had heard those words many times. *Money and material things aren't everything,* he had thought. But as usual he had said nothing.

Rob Bridges had been born in the village, and had become friends with Jack on the first day that they had met. They soon found that they had something in common: a complete disregard for other people's property or feelings. Both mothers blamed their antisocial activities on the other mother's son. Jack craved attention. But if his father wasn't going to supply it, then he would find other ways of making people take notice.

Jack had only been in the village for a few days, when he

first came to the notice of Police Constable Morton. Toby Morton wasn't exactly built for speed, more for comfort, but there was nothing wrong with his eyesight. He was checking the backs of some properties one evening when he saw Jack emerging from the yard of The Bull's Head.

"I'll take those," he said.

Jack tucked the two bottles of Coke inside his jacket and turned as if to run.

"No point doing that lad, it's Jack Fletcher isn't it?"

Jack was so surprised that the officer knew his name that he dropped one of the bottles, which split and emptied its contents over the floor.

"You can pay for that, when you return the other bottle," Toby said sternly. It must have been something to do with Toby Morton's demeanour, that convinced Jack it was a good idea to obey the officer, and to allow himself to be marched back to the public house, where he was made to apologize for his actions.

But if Toby Morton had thought that early detection would prevent any further incidents, he was sadly mistaken.

Over the following weeks Jack's activities became more and more anti–social, and adventurous; especially when he and Rob teamed up. Rob Bridges had always been on the verge of being out of his parents control. Jack wasn't always comfortable with his wrong doings, but he didn't want to appear weak. After all, just how many friends did he have?

The combined efforts of the two young tearaways also changed the habits of many of the male residents of the village. Where previously they had discussed farming, politics, and sport, now the dominant subject was the latest misdemeanour committed by the boys.

The subject of their wrongdoings cropped up yet again one stormy evening in the Bull's Head, over a pint or two of the local ale. It was Joe Richards who spoke first. "Something needs to be done about this new lad Fletcher, and young Bridges."

"You're not wrong Joe," Toby Morton added. He often popped into the pub for a quick pint after duty. With a coat over his uniform, and his tie in his pocket, he could relax, even though, as a village bobby he was seldom really off duty.

"What he needs is the influence of a good man, someone who will show him the values in life," Toby added.

"You shouldn't worry, something will turn up, it always does."

All heads turned. The voice had come from within the shadows near to the door.

"Allow me to introduce myself. Bartholomew Bussey at your service," the stranger said, as he stepped towards them.

Standing before them was a man of some sixty plus years. He was tall and slim. His hair was silver white in colour, and it was combed back. A thin moustache and goatee beard were neatly trimmed, and contrasted against his tanned face. He could not disguise his age, but his steel grey eyes sparkled with an inner brightness that held his audience entranced.

"I've just bought the old book shop," he said. "I'll be opening very soon."

"What another bookshop?" Joe asked.

"No something far more special; something for the good of the community."

"Can I get you something to drink?" Toby asked.

"No, but thank you; perhaps another time. I thought I would just call in to introduce myself. I bid you goodnight gentlemen." He smiled, turned, and was gone.

"Did you see an umbrella?" Joe asked no one in particular.

"Can't said as I did," replied Toby.

"But it's been raining heavily for the last half hour at least," Joe continued. "And he was bone dry!"

TWO

The Joys of Parenthood

Carol Fletcher knew instantly the phone rang that Paul wouldn't be coming home that night. It happened so regularly. She had even suspected him of having an affair, but he had denied that, and there was no evidence to support the theory.

"Hello love, I'm ever so sorry but I just won't be able to make it tonight."

"But you promised."

"I said I would try my best, I never promised."

"But you know how important this evening is."

"I know, but at least you'll be there. You can tell me what happened when I get back."

Carol Fletcher couldn't remember the last time that Paul had attended his son's school on parents evening. She hated parents evenings, she always had. With Paul Fletcher a virtual workaholic, there had been very few occasions when they had attended as a couple. Attending alone would have been bad enough, but to never hear anything positive about her son compounded the agony.

Her appointment with Jack's teacher was for seven fifteen. Carol spent more time than usual on her selection of clothes, and preparation. She would look good, even if she felt terrible.

As Carol Fletcher drove across country that evening, she reflected on her life. She was living in a village that didn't welcome newcomers, her husband was rarely at home, and her son was to all intents and purposes out of control.

The car park was almost full, but Carol found a space some distance from the main entrance. It was only the third time that she had visited this particular school, but her previous visits had left sufficient reference points in her memory.

"Good evening Mrs Fletcher, please take a seat."

"Thank you."

Mr Rawson was the Year Head at Jack's school. He reminded Carol Fletcher of a teacher that had taught her English many years back. He was a man in his late forties or early fifties. His dark brown hair was greying at the sides, and needed trimming. His tweed jacket had seen better days, and sported leather elbow patches. And he was a pipe smoker. He wasn't smoking at this time of course, but his old pipe was nestling safely in his top pocket.

"Well, where shall we start?" He said.

This doesn't bode well, she thought.

"Let's start with the positives. Jack is a regular attendee.

It's a fact that has quite surprised me. Bearing in mind his general behaviour, I would have thought that he would have missed the odd day."

Carol Fletcher gave a weak smile. *I suppose that's something*, she thought. There was a long pause. It was Carol that spoke next.

"Is that it Mr Rawson?"

"I'm afraid so."

"And the negatives?"

By the time that Carol Fletcher left the school, she was thoroughly depressed.

THREE

Top Gun

The next morning Jack woke with a start. He dressed quickly, and descended the stairs three at a time.

"Why didn't you wake me Mum, we're going to be late?"

"You had better speak to your Dad." She turned and busied herself spreading toast. Jack knew what was coming, it had happened so many times. Paul Fletcher folded his newspaper, and placed it carefully on the table. He was dressed in his blue pinstripe suit, white shirt and blue tie. It was pretty obvious that he wasn't going fishing.

"I'm sorry Jack, but I just have to go to an important business meeting."

"But you never said anything last night."

"I didn't get the phone call until late on. You were fast asleep by then."

"You should have woken me up, at least I wouldn't have got up this morning thinking I was late."

"I'm sorry son, I thought I was doing the right thing."

Jack turned to his mother. "I'll eat my breakfast in my room."

The look from his mother stopped Paul Fletcher from saying what he was about to say. Carol waited until Jack had left the room before she spoke again. She was obviously upset.

"It's just that we never see you."

"I'm doing it for us," Paul replied. "For our future."

"But what about Jack?"

"He's part of us, I meant all of us."

"But don't you think he'd like to spend some time with his father?"

"Things will get better, I'm just trying to secure our future."

"Do you think we have a future?"

"What do mean by that?"

"Well I don't know whether I can go on like this."

"I promise you, things will get better. We'll talk later."

Jack ate his toast in silence, and picked up his mobile phone. His right thumb moved quickly, and in no time at all he was pressing the appropriate button to send the message to Rob.

"Bye Jack," Paul Fletcher shouted from the hall. "I'll pick up that new phone you wanted whilst I'm out."

"Great," Jack replied. At that moment he couldn't have cared less about a new phone, he just wanted out of there.

As the BMW. slid quietly out of the drive, Jack descended the stairs and slipped out of the back door. He took his bike from the shed and headed for Rob's house.

Carol Fletcher switched on the kettle, and then switched it off again. It wasn't tea she really wanted, or needed at that moment. Of course, she wouldn't admit to herself that she had a drink problem, but then drinkers don't. It was just a bit of comfort, whilst Paul was away, she told herself.

Carol opened the large bottom drawer on the right hand side of her desk, and took out the bottle she had bought two days previously. There was just enough left to fill the small sherry glass that also resided in that drawer.

* * *

Edna Weatherall worked hard on her garden, she always had. When not in the garden she would be busy in her greenhouse. She spent hours planting individual seeds in small pots. Then even longer pricking them out, when they grew into seedlings, in order to re pot them. She always grew far too many, but derived great pleasure from giving them away. It had been some years since Newton Magna had won a prize in the area. Edna was determined that no criticism could be levelled at her. Certainly, if Newton Magna was to stand a chance of winning the area 'Village in Bloom' this year, there was work to be done. The early spring warmth had already produced some colour, with tulips and daffodils filling the front borders. As the weeks passed they would be replaced by the splendour of summer.

But the boys thought about the flowers in a completely different way. Jack broke open the barrel with his left hand, and dropped the lead pellet into the breech. With a metallic click he snapped the rifle shut, and settled into position, lying flat on the ground. The old oak tree served as both camouflage, and shade. Resting his left hand on his school bag, he allowed the cross-hairs of the telescopic sight to settle on the target. Jack half breathed out, then held his breath before squeezing the trigger. There was a dull crack, and another of Mrs Weatherall's beautiful tulips was decapitated.

"That's eighteen, just two to go," Jack said, as he loaded the air rifle for his next shot.

"I told you it was a good gun didn't I?" His companion in crime said, as Jack settled for what he hoped would be the penultimate shot.

But things don't always go as planned. Yes he lined the shot up perfectly, but what he had failed to do was check the back-stop. The other shots, having de-flowered the garden, had disappeared quietly into the soft earth of the raised bed behind. Directly behind this tulip was the metal pole of Mrs Weatherall's rotary dryer.

The shot sent the tulip head tumbling, but the noise that followed as the pellet glanced off the pole, and hit the metal water tub, brought the owner rushing from her back door.

The sight of the bare flower stalks stopped her dead. The look of initial total disbelief quickly changed to an angry scowl.

"Don't you be thinking I don't know who's done this," she shouted. "You'll get your just deserts, believe you me."

Jack and Rob slid from their spot, and ran across the

nearby field. They didn't stop running until they reached the shelter of Butcher's Bridge on the nearby canal.

"I told you we'd have some fun," Rob said, as he took back the rifle, and slipped it neatly into its cover. "Ben will never know it's been out of his room."

Ben was Rob's older brother. The Bridges lived next door but one to Jack in London Road. The houses were exactly the same in design, being three bedroomed semi–detached. There were five pairs in total, all being completed in nineteen thirty. On the opposite side of the road stood terraced houses built over forty years previously.

Jack was an only child. He lived at number 9 with his parents Carol and Paul Fletcher, although Paul spent much of his time, away from home, on business. Jack didn't really like that. Getting presents whenever his father returned helped to compensate to some small degree, but in truth this was no real substitute for the close relationship that Jack would have liked to have had with his dad. What he also lacked was discipline, or a respect for other people's property, especially since teaming up with Rob Bridges.

During the eighteen months that he had been in the village Jack had received numerous police cautions, and had even been threatened with a custodial sentence. It would have been wise to listen to P.C. Morton, there was more to him than met the eye. Toby Morton had taken and passed his exams for promotion to Sergeant, but a prank that went wrong, whilst on a training course, had blotted his copybook. Toby wasn't present at the time, and had taken no part in the incident, but he had been tarred with the same brush as all the others on the course. He had requested the move to Newton Magna, to distance himself from the others. He hoped that one day he would be looked upon more favourably.

FOUR

Rebel Without A Cause

Most youngsters have favourite places, where they like to go, either to meet friends, or to have time to themselves. Jack's favourite spot was by the lock on the canal.

It was early spring, and a few boats were to be seen on the canal. Jack liked to watch the various crews work through the locks, especially when they were obviously inexperienced. There was a hire base some miles further north, and Newton Locks were the first locks that some boaters had ever encountered.

As Jack sat on the black and white seat, that the then British Waterways had seen fit to place alongside the bottom lock, he watched a hire boat approaching. Two women seemed to be enjoying the countryside, sitting with their feet up, at the front of the boat, glasses in hand. At the rear were two men, and two young children.

Their approach was steady, in fact so steady that it

seemed as though the boat would never arrive. Eventually the steerer brought the boat nearer to the towpath, and his mate walked along the side of the boat. He seemed full of confidence. But when the boat hit the bank with a heavy thud, it very nearly caused him to be thrown into the water. Somehow though he managed to hold on. Next he stepped off, and held the bow in to the bank by use of the rope. The problem was, the wind had by now made its presence felt, and blown the stern across the canal. When the steerer threw his rope towards his mate on the tow–path, in an attempt to recover the situation, it fell short and dropped into the water. Without thinking about the possible consequences, the man at the controls put on some power, to straighten the boat up. The trailing rope found the propeller, and disappeared like a jet propelled water snake. There was an almighty bang, and the engine stopped. Jack couldn't stop laughing. This was one of the best episodes that he had witnessed. But when he noticed that the man on the bank had seen him laughing, he decided that it would be a good idea to move on.

Jack hadn't always been this way. In fact, up to the time of moving to Newton Magna he had been 'quite a pleasant young man'. It was hard to say why he had changed so much. His father blamed his hormones. His mother blamed the long hours that his father worked. The truth was more complicated. Whilst his physical changes played their part, and the lack of his father's presence also took its toll, it had been the move away from London that had been the catalyst for the transformation.

Jack had been quite excited when they first bought

the house in the village. There would be somewhere to go in the school holidays, when his friends were away as, 'normal' family holidays had been put on hold. His father being just too busy with some deal or other. When 9 London Road became their family home, Jack's opinion of the house and location changed dramatically. He felt as though he had been betrayed. At thirteen Jack considered that he was old enough to have a say in family matters. Unfortunately, in the Fletcher household, democracy didn't exist, Jack wasn't allowed a vote.

The first boy of the same age that Jack met after the move was Rob Bridges. Rob was only too happy to recruit a fellow rebel.

FIVE

A Glass Act

They had planned it over two weeks previously; it was to be their finest hour. The incident with the tulips had been fun, and they had enjoyed burning down Mr King's garden shed. It had served him right for being a busybody. But now even shoplifting had lost its appeal. They had decided that all they had done previously was kid's stuff. Breaking into Old Man Riley's house would put them in the big league.

Mr Riley lived alone in the Old Lock Cottage by the canal. He was fiercely independent, and never asked for help, even though these days he walked very slowly, and with a pronounced stoop. He ventured out just once a week, on pension day. He would leave the Cottage at precisely nine thirty in the morning, and push his four wheel trolley to the Old Post Office and general store. There he would collect his money, and purchase everything he needed. The milkman delivered his milk, bread, and potatoes. From the old man's appearance, it seemed that he didn't have 'two pennies to rub together', but there were rumours that the cottage housed items of value.

Jack and Rob watched the front door, from the hedge on the far side of the canal. At nine thirty precisely the door opened. The battered tartan trolley appeared first, and then the bent figure of Mr Riley, complete with tweed jacket and cloth cap.

"Told you he'd be on time," Rob whispered.

Jack didn't answer, but watched nervously as the old man made his way along the towpath towards the nearby bridge.

Jack checked in both directions. There was no one in sight. He clambered over the lock gates, holding tightly to the white painted rail.

The single pane of glass was the original, barely four millimetres thick. Jack could see the interior of the kitchen. There was an old table, complete with plastic table cloth, an old white sink, and on the draining board, a single cup, saucer and plate. Jack took one last look around and then turned his back to the door. It was all so easy. A quick jab with his right elbow, and the glass gave way. Even the key had been left on the inside. Jack slipped his left hand passed the fragments of broken glass, turned the lock, and was inside in moments.

Outside, Rob was well hidden. He had a full view of the surrounding area, but it was unlikely that anyone would spot him, deep in the laurel bush. In his right hand was a referee's whistle. Small but capable of emitting a very loud warning signal.

Twenty minutes later, amidst a cloud of cigarette smoke, the boys examined their loot.

"Is that all there was?" Rob growled, before taking another long drag on his cigarette. "Hardly worth the effort."

"That's rich coming from you, it was me that took the risks," Jack snapped.

"Everybody thought he was worth a few bob, how was I to know the old duffer had nothing but junk," Rob said as he dropped the medals into the bag.

"Can't we sell those?" Jack asked.

"What, and get arrested within hours. We're not exactly well connected are we?"

"I suppose you're right," Jack conceded.

"Still ten quid is ten quid. We'll dump the rest." Rob smiled as he pushed the note into his pocket.

"Hey."

"Don't worry, we'll split it later."

They finished their cigarettes, and headed along the canal tow path. As they cycled under the turnover bridge Rob tossed the bag containing the medals into the water. It disappeared in an instant into the inky blackness.

* * *

"What time do you call this?" Mrs Fletcher yelled, as Jack stepped quietly into the Kitchen. The house had been in darkness.

"Thought I was in bed did you?"

The answer was of course yes.

"Go on, explain yourself."

Jack could tell that his mother was in no mood for lies.

"I've just been out and about with Rob. We just lost track of time."

"Rob Bridges again."

"He's all right."

"So you're the bad influence then are you?"

"We were just having a bit of fun."

"No doubt at somebody else's expense."

"Can't I just go to bed?" Jack asked, hoping that his mother would be in a better mood by morning. She usually was.

"No you can't. Not until I've finished."

Jack slumped back into one of the chairs.

"The trouble is Jack, you've had it too easy. It's about time that you worked for what you get. Perhaps you would appreciate things more." Jack realized that this wasn't the time to tell his mother that he had split his new trainers. He would wait until his dad came home, he was a soft touch. He never said no.

"You'll be telling me next that people of my age used to have to work for a living," Jack mumbled.

They had had this self same conversation many times.

"Well they used to years ago, and it didn't do them any harm."

"Here we go, the good old days."

"I'm not saying that things were necessarily better, but at least people respected others more."

"Yeah, yeah, yeah," Jack muttered.

"Oh, get to bed, I don't know what I'm going to do with you."

Jack thought about what his mother had said, but not for long.

SIX

Bold as Brass

The boys' money didn't last long. The price of cigarettes saw to that. It was now a matter of planning the next money making scheme. It was as they were mentally pondering their next move, that they found themselves standing outside the new 'second hand shop', in the High Street.

The gold lettering on the window announced –

BUSSEY'S EMPORIUM
KNICK – KNACKS AND ARTIFACTS
Proprietor – Bartholomew Bussey

There was nothing in the window that particularly interested them, but they found themselves drawn towards the door. They were soon looking through the various items that filled the shop. Jack picked up a belt that was made of thick brown leather. It had a highly polished brass buckle, and although somewhat old fashioned, looked brand new. Keeping his back to the shopkeeper, Jack wound up the belt and slipped it into his coat pocket. He then moved slowly towards the door. Rob had helped himself to a silver cigarette case, which he had slid into his trouser pocket, whilst using Jack as cover.

"Come back and see me sometime soon," Mr Bussey called, as they stepped out of the shop and onto the pavement.

By the time that the shopkeeper had reached the door, Jack was running as fast as he could towards the canal, and Rob had sauntered off along the street, his hands thrust deep in his pockets. Mr Bussey smiled, and stepped back into his shop.

Jack was still running when his feet hit the towpath, and he headed under the old road bridge. The high-pitched whistle of a train passing through nearby Market Clayton stopped him in his tracks. He could see the mix of smoke and steam behind the line of trees in the distance.

His heart was thumping now. Not from the effort of the run. No, he was fit enough; he had to be. He must have imagined it; it just couldn't be real. He bent forward to catch his breath, resting his hands on his thighs. What he saw threatened to stop his heart altogether.

Gone were his expensive trainers. In their place were heavy brown boots. And in place of his jeans, thick wool trousers. Jack dropped to his knees, and looked at his reflection in the dark still water. Yes it was the same face, but everything else had changed, his shirt; his jacket. He glanced at his left wrist. His watch was no longer there, and there was no mark to show where it had been. There was only one thing to do. He turned and retraced his steps. Perhaps Mr Bussey could help.

But it wasn't only Jack's clothes that had changed. Very little of Newton Magna, as he knew it, was there any more. The street signs were different, there was quiet, and a lack of vehicles. Busseys was no longer there. In fact all that row of shops had gone. There were just houses in the High Street.

Jack ran as fast as his legs would carry him, he had to get home. He stopped at the corner of High Street and London Road. He hardly dare go on, just what would he find? No matter what, he had to know.

As he slowly inched forward, and London Road lay before him, his worst fears were realized. The row of small terraced houses, built long ago in the Victorian age, stood proudly basking in the what was now evening sunlight. But it had been years since they had warmed themselves thus. The houses opposite, which included Jack's at number 9, had robbed their older companions of the beauty of a sunset. But where number 9, London Road should have been, only foundations now stood, surrounded by weeds.

The front door of one of the terraced houses opened, and a young boy of no more than ten years stepped onto the pavement. He wore brown laced boots, and knee length socks, one of which was down. Over his shirt was a brown sleeveless pullover. His cheeks were full and rosy, his hair dark brown, and loosely tousled.

Jack's instinct was to run across to the boy, he had so

many questions, but he was fearful of scaring him. Instead he called out

"Hello there, can you help me?"

The boy walked toward him slowly. He had no trouble crossing the road, it was deserted. It was surreal somehow with no vehicles anywhere. Jack didn't wait until the boy reached him, he couldn't wait, his mind was spinning.

"What's happened to all the houses?" Jack blurted out.

"What houses?" the boy replied.

"These houses." Jack pointed at the low brick footings, and neat squares of weeds.

"Nothing's happened, how could it, they haven't been built yet?"

The boy turned to walk away.

"Just a minute," Jack half shouted. "What's the date?"

"The nineteenth," the boy said, his face a human question mark.

"No, the year?" Jack was becoming frantic.

"Nineteen thirty." The boy shook his head, and began to run back to his house. The front door slammed shut. Wherever he had intended to go could wait until later.

Jack's legs began to tremble. He just had to sit down. There could be no other explanation for what had happened. He had somehow travelled through time to nineteen thirty; a time when even his mother and father had not been born. But how was that possible? He had no answers, and he certainly wouldn't find any in his present location.

SEVEN

Rob Boy

Rob had walked no more than half a mile from the shop when his feet suddenly felt heavy. He had heard the same train whistle that Jack had heard, but had dismissed it out of hand. Of course he hadn't seen the steam and smoke. He looked down.

"What the xxxx?" he exclaimed. For not only had his bright white trainers gone, being replaced by a scruffy pair of lace up boots, but his faded jeans had also been changed into baggy brown cords.

He ran to the nearest house, and gasped as he saw his reflection in the window. And as the focal length of his eyes changed he found that he was now looking through the glass, and into the room beyond. There was no television, just an old radio on a sideboard. The furniture was similar to that he had seen in a living museum, and the floor was covered in linoleum, with several old rugs thereon.

Quickly moving to the next of the terraced houses he held his hands to the side of his face, and peered in. The room was very similar to the first house, with the addition of an upright piano. He looked about him, and studied the scene. There were no television aerials, no satellite dishes, and no yellow lines on the road. Everything he knew had changed.

Rob spun round as he heard the sound of horse's hooves on the cobble stones. It was as the horse and cart were driven by that he realized that the road surface in his day was tarmacadam.

There was no rational explanation for his next move; he just ran. And he didn't stop running until he saw the church. Overgrown and neglected in his day, now neat and tidy, with various floral displays. His heart was thumping, and his mind racing as he started to check the gravestones. He found the latest date to be 1930, and that headstone appeared new; the grave being the last of the line on the eastern perimeter of the graveyard. There was a notice board immediately outside the church, bearing a number of notices. There were several yellowed sheets, dated 1929, and a crisp, fresh notice concerning services for 1930. Rob turned, and shouted at the top of his voice, "Noooooooooo!" And as he did so, the door to the church opened, and an elderly churchman appeared, wearing a white 'dog collar' and black robe.

"Can I help you son?" he asked as Rob stood frozen to the spot; the colour drained from his face.

"This isn't real, is it?" Rob managed to say, after taking a deep breath.

"What isn't?" Replied the churchman.

"I mean, it can't be," Rob babbled.

"I don't understand, young man, is there something you don't understand?"

"Yes there is, just tell me what year it is, will you?"

"What year? Why it's nineteen thirty of course. Are you feeling ill?"

But Rob wasn't ill, unless you count severe shock as an illness.

"Come inside young man, you had better sit down."

"No no, I'm all right," and with those words Rob took to his heals again, although he hadn't a clue as to where he was heading.

He was still running when he came across a greengrocers shop. A thriving business in nineteen thirty; long gone before Rob was born. A thought flashed through his mind. *No problem here, no one knows who I am.* Looking about him, he quickly grabbed a bunch of bananas, and several apples, which he stuffed inside his shirt, and walked briskly away.

"Hey, you little thief," the shopkeeper shouted after him, having seen the theft through the shop window.

Fat lot you can do, Rob thought, as he smiled to himself, gave the shopkeeper a two finger salute, and disappeared round the corner.

EIGHT

A Room For The Night

Jack couldn't remember how he came to be on the outskirts of Market Clayton. He had just started walking, without any idea of what he was going to do next. After all he was in deep shock. He thought about having a cigarette, but his pockets were now empty. Even the leather belt he had stolen had disappeared.

The first indication of the existence of the village in his day was always the derelict station building. Jack had played there so many times since moving into the area. But this time it was different; the building was no longer in poor condition.

The approach was clean and tidy, with well-manicured hedgerows and a railed gate that had the fresh smell of creosote. Even the name board was freshly painted, and proudly announced that the station was part of the London Midland and Scottish Railway. Jack opened the gate and walked through to the platform.

It was like stepping into an old film. At the far end of the platform a porter was attending to parcels on a three wheeled trolley. An elderly lady, wearing a fur coat and large hat, was sitting on a wrought iron seat enjoying the last of the evening sunshine. At each end of the platform neat and colourful flower beds showed the pride that the staff had in their work. The single track, complete with wooden sleepers, was completely devoid of weeds. The ballast stones were even and neatly edged, and the polished steel rails indicated frequent use.

Beyond the main line there were a number of sidings containing large numbers of assorted goods wagons, many with the letters L. M. S. thereon.

As Jack stood there taking it all in, there was a clunk, as a signal arm lifted, and he heard the shrill sound of a train whistle a short distance away. Within moments a small black steam locomotive, hauling four maroon carriages pulled into the station. Doors opened, the porter loaded the parcels, and the elderly lady was assisted into a compartment by the guard who had stepped from the train.

Jack remained motionless as the scene was played out. The porter had completed his loading, and assisted with the door closing. The guard checked that all was well, took note of the 'all right signal' from the porter, waved his green flag above his head, and stepped onto the train. The driver, who had been looking back from the footplate, pulled his head in, blew the whistle and restarted his journey.

The locomotive moved gently forward with scarcely a

sound, and then there was a loud bark as the first exhausts from the cylinders rushed from the chimney. As the train accelerated away the sounds came rapidly, one after another. The sound of the piston beats could be heard well into the distance, and all that was left was the smell of steam, coal, and warm oil. As the porter returned to his office, Jack slipped quietly away, returned to the roadway, and continued his trek towards Market Clayton.

The village was much quieter than the last time that Jack had been there. There was a lack of traffic for a start, and he could even hear a blackbird singing in a nearby tree. His eyes scanned the roofs of the first houses. There were no television aerials, no satellite dishes, everywhere seemed neater somehow.

But if this village was also in nineteen thirty, there was nowhere that he could go, no one that he knew. He needed time to think, somewhere to plan his next move, but where? There was only one place he could think of that would afford him shelter, and privacy.

Within ten minutes he had climbed the fence at the rear of the goods yard, and was checking to find an insecure door. Fifteen wagons later he succeeded.

Other than a musty smell the interior was clean, and although there was nothing but floorboards on which to lay, Jack soon curled up in a corner, and despite his confused mind was asleep in moments.

NINE

Unhappy Return

The house was in darkness when Paul Fletcher returned. Carol Fletcher was asleep at her desk. The empty sherry glass was on the floor beneath her right hand. The laptop had long since shut down to standby mode, having been idle for some considerable time. Paul took the sherry glass away, made some strong coffee, and woke his wife.

"I'm sorry," she said, as Paul handed her the coffee.

"What's this all about?" He said, as he dropped into his favourite chair.

"It's just that I'm so lonely. You're always working, and Jack's got his friends."

"I didn't realize you were so low."

"I know I shouldn't be," she said. "We've got a lovely house, and money's no problem, but I wish we could spend more time together."

"We will, we will, I'm just so tied up at work at the moment."

"But Paul, money isn't everything. What was it someone once said? Better to live in a tent on the beach, with someone you love, than to live in a mansion by yourself. Well it was something like that."

Paul put down his coffee, and moved over to the settee, to be with his wife. He took her in his arms and held her tight.

"You're right, we need to sort a few things out."

Carol Fletcher rested her head on her husband's shoulder and sobbed gently.

"Come on love, let's go to bed," Paul said. "Things will look better in the morning. How's Jack by the way, is he all right?"

"Jack," she exclaimed. "I'd forgotten all about Jack. He must be in bed."

They climbed the stairs together, and looked into Jack's room. The bed was empty, and hadn't been disturbed.

"He must be at Rob's," Carol said.

"But surely he would have let you know?"

"Perhaps he tried to, and I missed the call."

"Perhaps nothing, I think we had better check."

It was Mr Bridges who answered the telephone, after some considerable delay.

"Hello," he said. It was pretty obvious from his voice that he had been asleep.

"I'm very sorry to disturb you Mr Bridges, but this is Paul Fletcher, Jack's dad. I was just making sure that Jack was stopping at your house tonight."

"But I thought they had arranged to stay at your house. If they're not there, then I don't know where they are."

"You say they, you mean Rob isn't at home?"

"No, that's what I said. I thought that they were at your house."

There was an uneasy silence. It was Ray Bridges who spoke next.

"I'll get hold of Toby Morton, he'll know what to do."

Paul Fletcher replaced the receiver and turned to his wife. "Carol, he's not there."

"What do you mean, he's not there?"

"Rob's not there either, Rob's dad is ringing the police."

"You mean Toby Morton?"

"I suppose so."

"And what next?"

"We wait, what else can we do?"

The phone was just into its second ring when Paul Fletcher snatched it up.

"Hello, Paul Fletcher here."

"Good evening Mr Fletcher." It was the unmistakable voice of Toby Morton.

"I'm at Mr and Mrs Bridge's house at the moment, I'll be with you as quickly as possible. In the meantime, could you write down a list of anywhere you think he might have gone. And an up to date photograph would be very useful."

"What did he say?" Carol Fletcher asked, the moment Paul put down the phone.

Paul Fletcher repeated the conversation word for word.

"He'll be fine love. After all, where could two boys go in this village?"

***

Toby Morton arrived about thirty minutes later.

"I'm sorry to have kept you," he said as he removed his cap. His helmet was only used when he was walking around the village.

"I've got what information I could from Mr and Mrs Bridges, which to be honest isn't a lot. I'm hoping that you'll be able to throw some light on the matter."

Carol Fletcher handed him a mug of tea, for which he thanked her, and sat down next to her husband. They held hands, and it was clear to see that they were extremely concerned.

"When did you last see Jack?" Toby asked.

"It was this morning, just after Paul went off to a meeting. I'm sure he was going to meet Rob Bridges."

"That ties up with what they told me. Rob got a text message, presumably from your lad, and left the house almost immediately."

"What do we do now?" Asked Paul Fletcher. "Shouldn't we be out looking for them?"

"Not a lot we can really do in the dark, Mr Fletcher. But I've organized some more manpower for the morning. We're meeting at first light."

"I'd like to help," Paul said. "I suppose Carol had better stay here in case he comes home, or makes contact?"

"You've got it, Mr Fletcher. I've made the same arrangement with Mr and Mrs Bridges."

Toby Morton finished the last of his tea, after completing the Missing Person Form, and with a photograph of Jack safely tucked inside his document case, wished them goodnight.

TEN

Constable's Country

A large personnel carrier pulled up outside the Police House where Toby Morton was ready and waiting. Sergeant Bill Parker was in charge of the unit, and after a short conversation with Toby, he briefed his officers.

"Now I know I'm the Sergeant, but Toby here knows this area like the back of his hand. Whilst on this operation, he'll be second in charge, and responsible for briefings and liaison with the local community. I shall give him all the assistance I can, and deal with any press that may become involved."

Toby's face visibly flushed. Perhaps here was his opportunity to show his worth. The moment he had been waiting for since he had transferred.

Paul Fletcher and Ray Bridges stood waiting at the gate to Toby's house.

"Don't stand there, come in and join us," Toby said.

The responsibility he now had was reflected in the authoritative tone. The photographs were passed around, and Toby told them what he knew. He then introduced the two fathers to the police contingent. He was determined that they would be involved fully in the police operation.

***

It made sense to search the more obvious places first. People knew far more about the boys than Jack and Rob realized. Toby Morton even had his own intelligence file, which he passed to Sergeant Parker to use to plan his strategy.

Toby knew that the canal towpath was the favourite haunt for the two boys. The possibility of an accident could not be ruled out.

In an attempt to minimize the disruption to early season holiday makers that were using the canal, Toby had met up with Canal and River Trust staff before dawn. He had watched as they partially drained each section of water in turn. The search was of course negative, as all searches would be.

After this operation, Toby just had enough time for a cup of tea, and a quick simple breakfast before Sergeant Parker and his team arrived. By late morning, virtually the whole village had joined the search for the boys. Those that were less mobile helped in whatever way they could. Mrs Blewitt, a leading member of The Royal Voluntary Service in the area, rallied her troops and took over the village hall.

Alf Parsons had unlocked the building, and was hovering around hoping to taste the various delights.

"You can keep your hands off those sandwiches," he was told in no uncertain terms by Margaret Bishop. The size of the bread knife in her hand seemed, in some way, to emphasize the point.

"Just looking, Mrs Bishop, you're doing a grand job. Must say the grub looks good."

"Refreshments, Mr Parsons, refreshments."

"Sorry Mrs Bishop," said Alf.

"Well make yourself useful man," said Mrs Blewitt, who was standing nearby. "Go and fetch another of those tea urns."

ELEVEN

Sidetracked

Pat Jardine and Ernie Rogers arrived at the yard within a few moments of each other. Pat was on his new black Raleigh cycle, which he kept immaculately clean. The chrome wheel rims reflected the yard lights as he lifted it into the rack, and locked it securely. It wasn't so much theft that bothered him, as that was unlikely in this area. It was the fear of having it removed, and hidden somewhere as a joke by some of the pranksters that concerned him most. Ernie didn't have to bother. After all, no one would take his battered and rusting old wreck.

Pat had been with the railway since the end of his school days, only leaving for a short while during the Great War, in order to fight for his beloved Country. He needn't have gone, being in a reserved occupation, but the death of his older brother in France had prompted him to enlist. He had returned to the railway at the end of hostilities.

Ernie was still in his teens, and had been Pat's fireman for the last ten months. They got on well together, almost like father and son. They had their moments, of course, but that was only to be expected.

"Morning Pat, how's the back?"

"Not too good really, but keep it quiet. Don't want everyone knowing, else they'll have me on the sick."

"I suppose you want me to oil up then?"

"If you're offering. I'll check her over first though."

They'd got their usual small, black tank engine, which was ideal for shunting, and short trips down the line. Not for them the luxury of stepping onto the footplate of an already prepared locomotive. Preparation, oiling, and all the other little jobs before moving off, was down to them.

Pat didn't feel guilty, letting his mate climb about underneath to reach the various oiling points, that was how he'd learned his trade some years back. There was no quick way to becoming a driver. Everyone started at the bottom, as a cleaner, or sometimes a knocker–up. It was some time before they progressed to fireman, and eventually to driver. Even then the procedure could be painfully slow. When they sometimes visited the larger stations, Ernie would watch the expresses go by, with misty eyes, dreaming of the day when he would be at the controls of such trains as the Mid–Day Scot.

"You'll get there, lad," Pat had said. "Provided that you keep your nose clean, and work hard."

Many a time they had discussed the subject, and each time Pat had said the same thing. "If something's worth having, it's worth waiting and working for."

Ernie had set his goal, and nothing was going to stop him achieving it.

With the preparation done, and the fire burning through, Pat opened his bag, and removed a parcel wrapped in grease proof paper. He had washed the firing shovel using the slacking pipe. The scalding water having removed any deposits that were lingering on the blade. He unwrapped the paper, took a lump of lard and placed it on the shovel. He rested the blade partway into the firebox, and the lard melted instantly. Next came two sausages, which he placed on the shovel. He waited until they began to brown, turning them with a knife, before cracking an egg into the fat. Ernie took a cheese sandwich from his canvas shoulder bag.

"Don't worry lad, I'll save you a bit of fat to dip your bread in," Pat said, as he prised the egg from the shovel.

Most mornings in the goods yard followed this pattern, Pat with his fry up, and Ernie getting to dip his bread. It was on one such occasion that they had almost come to blows. Ernie had totally forgotten about Pat's fry up, and had adjusted the blower valve in an attempt to raise the steam pressure. The effect was immediate. The blower not only drew the fire, it also succeeded in sucking Pat's breakfast from the shovel. Ernie had dropped down from the footplate instantly, and didn't return until some time had passed.

Pat checked his pocket watch.

"Time to move," he said. "You can have another go this morning. See if you can be a bit more gentle this time."

Ernie eased open the regulator, and steam at over a

hundred pounds per square inch shot from the front of the engine. Very slowly the wheels began to turn, and a muffed bark came from the chimney. They were on their way.

They topped up the tanks at the water tower and moved to the far end of the yard. The shunters were waiting for them, long shunting poles held aloft like pikestaffs in their hands.

"Need them out of three road first," Charlie Moore shouted, as the locomotive came to a stop. "Take 'em straight up to Waverly's Cross, will you?"

"Right Charlie," Pat replied. "Better watch yourselves, Ernie's at the controls."

There was no comment from Ernie, he was used to Pat's sense of humour. Even at five miles per hour, eighty tons can cause some damage. The buffers met with a thump, and several wagons moved backward as the shock of the impact travelled along the siding.

Jack woke with a jolt, literally. He had just managed to get to his feet when the second jolt came. It was more severe, and he found himself on the floor once again. The wagons were on the move. In a panic he reached to open the door. But it was no use, in the half light of the wagon's interior, it took him some considerable time to find the catch. By the time that he had, and succeeded in partially opening the heavy door, the train was moving too quickly for him to consider jumping clear. As the train picked up speed, Jack sat cross legged in the middle of the floor and stared out.

From his wooden hide, Jack watched the countryside go by. But it wasn't the countryside that he knew. Motor vehicles were few and far between, as were houses. Horses were to be seen in many parts, pulling wagons of different shapes and sizes. Men worked in the fields with little sign of mechanical help. And at most of the small stations that they passed through, silver coloured milk churns were gathered, having either been delivered, or were awaiting collection.

It suddenly dawned on Jack, just how hungry he was. But where or how could he get food? He had no money. He only had one skill, if you could call it that, the ability to steal. He was understandably nervous about starting his new life in this way, but what else could he do? And the sooner the better.

After what seemed an age the train began to slow. Jack took a quick look ahead, hoping that no one would see him. They were approaching a signal that was at danger. Without hesitating Jack prepared to jump. He double-checked that there was nothing in the way, and dropped down from the train just before it came to a standstill.

He hid in the trees until the signal lifted, and the goods train disappeared from view. Jack slipped away from the railway and into his next problem; just where was he?

All around him was farmland, with not a building in sight. Perhaps he should have stayed on the train. After all, sooner or later, it would have arrived somewhere with signposts.

What Jack didn't realize, was the significance of that red signal where he had left the train. Only a short distance along the line was another station, on the outskirts of a small town.

Jack, totally unaware of this information, started across the first field. He was thirsty, as well as hungry, and needed to find somewhere soon. By the time that he spotted the farm building his throat was parched. He didn't know what he was going to say, but he was going to say something.

There was a long delay before someone answered his knock. He stepped back, as the large wooden door was opened.

"Yes, what can I do for you young man?"

Standing before him was a large woman, probably in her forties, with a ruddy complexion, and hands that were covered in flour.

"I'm sorry to disturb you, but do you think I could please have a glass of water?"

"I think we can do better than that, come in and shut the door. I'm just doing a bit of cooking."

Jack stepped inside, wiped his boots on the mat, and waited.

"Well don't just stand out there you daft devil. There's nought out there to eat."

Jack had to admit that the smell of freshly baked bread was driving his taste buds wild.

The kitchen was huge. Standing in the centre of the room was a long, heavy wooden table, with high back chairs on both sides. The floor was of red flagstone tiles; that were polished and spotless. The cooking range was black and in similar condition.

"Well sit down young'un, eggs and bacon all right?"

"Err yes, thank you."

"They call me Beth, what name do you answer to?"

"Jack."

"That's a good strong name."

Beth took the enormous frying pan from the range, and placed two eggs, and three rashers of bacon onto an enamel plate. She then cut two enormous slices from a loaf that was cooling on a wire tray.

"Help yourself to butter lad."

Jack was even more hungry than he thought, eggs and bacon and warm slices of home-made bread were most welcome.

"Well now you've had the chance to fill your belly lad, perhaps you can tell me what brought you here."

"I needed a drink of water," Jack replied. He was deliberately trying to be evasive, without appearing to be rude.

"No, I mean these parts; where are you from?"

"Newton Magna."

"Can't say as I've heard of that, must be some distance away."

"Quite a way."

"Go on then son, how did you end up here?"

"I fell asleep in a railway wagon."

"That was a bit daft wasn't it?"

"I suppose it was."

"Better get you sorted out for getting home then. Bill will take you down the station when he gets back. I should think your parents will be worried sick. It's a shame that we don't have a telephone."

"But I haven't got any money to pay for a ticket."

"I realize that you silly sausage, else you'd have got on the next train back, wouldn't you?"

Jack gave a weak smile.

"Still never mind, we'll lend you the money, and you can post it to us when you get home. How does that sound?"

"Thank you," Jack replied.

But what good would that do? He thought. If Bill took him to the station, bought him a ticket and saw him off, he'd be back to square one at Market Clayton. And there was nothing for him there. In fact there was nothing for him anywhere. The awful reality of his situation was beginning to dawn on him. What if there was no way back to his own time, how would he survive? But then he was fit and agile, perhaps he could get a job somewhere. In nineteen thirty, boys of his age went to work. He knew that, as he'd heard the phrase from his mother so many times. But he would need somewhere to live as well, and he couldn't afford that. The accommodation would have to come with the job. It was the only answer.

Bill was a rough and ready sort of chap, but he was good hearted, and didn't hesitate when Beth told him the story.

"Right lad," he said. "I'll have me breakfast when I gets back. Your needs are greater than mine, and there's a train due soon."

Jack smiled and nodded. *Market Clayton, here I come,* he thought. It was another new experience for Jack, travelling in a horse drawn cart. But it took him considerable less time to reach the station at Waverley's

Cross than it had to reach the farm from where he had alighted from the train earlier.

With a note in his pocket, of Beth and Bill's address, and a promise that he would reimburse them for their kindness, Jack started his journey back. It was certainly more comfortable travelling in a carriage compared with a goods wagon.

***

Jack didn't remember much of the walk back to Newton Magna, he seemed to just walk on automatic pilot. Before he realized it, he was sitting on the balance beam of the old lock. Something had drawn him back to the canal.

TWELVE

A Rude Awakening

Rob woke with a start. *What a dream,* he thought, as he took a deep breath. But then reality kicked in. Not only was he laying on bare boards, but he saw scattered about him apple cores and banana skins from the previous day. *Can't live on fruit – can't stay here. And where is here?* Then he remembered breaking the rear window of an empty house. *No good staying here – I'm off to the Smoke.*

But as Rob sat thinking, it dawned on him that, if this was nineteen thirty, then the railway would still be here. All he had to do was hitch a ride! Now that whistle he had heard the day before made sense.

***

When the train stopped, Rob noticed that the carriages were similar to some that he had seen at a preserved railway the previous summers; lots of compartments, with no corridor.

Doors were closed, a flag was waved, and the driver responded with a toot from the whistle. Rob timed it perfectly. As the guard turned towards the door of his guards' compartment, Rob ran across the platform, opened the door, and was safely inside before the train had picked up to more than walking pace. Now he sat alone, with a broad grin on his face. *This is going to be easy,* he thought.

The train was a stopping passenger service, and progress was for Rob frustratingly slow. At station after station the train would stop; but no one joined him in his compartment.

By the time that he train reached the main line station Rob was hungry and thirsty. But getting to London was the goal; if he had to go without for a while then so be it.

***

He boarded the London bound train in the same manner as before, but this time there was a corridor. This time he would have to stay alert in order to avoid the officials, as he had neither ticket, nor the money to purchase one.

Compared to the other passengers in his compartment, Rob looked shabby, and out of place. He noticed that several of those travelling with him appeared uncomfortable in his presence. As the countryside flashed by, he leaned back, and closed his eyes. He was sound asleep almost immediately.

It was probably the smell of cigar smoke that woke him. This combined with the thud of the compartment door closing. But whatever it was, the timing was perfect, as Rob heard the words "tickets please," nearby. He was out of his seat, and into the corridor like lightning. He could hear a conversation taking place in the adjacent compartment. Luckily the toilet was vacant. But how long would he need to stay there?

***

Rob no longer had a watch or mobile phone, and therefore could not tell just how much time had passed whilst he had sat patiently waiting. But he knew that the train had been well into its journey when he had vacated the compartment in such haste. Then another thought flashed through his mind– *how do I get out of the station at London without a ticket?* He would have to leave the train before it reached its destination. Easier said than done when the train is a non–stopper.

Opening the door slowly, he checked the corridor in both directions; it was clear. But what he had planned necessitated the finding of an empty compartment.

Rob had just about conceded defeat when he found what he had been looking for. Without hesitation he slipped into the compartment, and moved to the far side. There he reached up, gripped the communication chain, and pulled it hard. He was somewhat surprised that the train did not squeal to a stop as he had expected.

On the footplate of the locomotive, Bill Penny reacted without delay to the sudden drop on the vacuum gauge. It had dropped rapidly from twenty one inches to eleven inches. He immediately flicked open the large ejector valve to restore the vacuum to the correct level, whilst at the same time taking into account the line ahead. Working as a team, fireman Terry Prichard opened the blower valve to draw the fire in preparation for the imminent closure of the regulator. Having satisfied himself that there were no unsuitable hazards ahead, Bill Penny closed the regulator, and applied the brakes in such a manner that the train would come to as rapid a stop as possible whilst maintaining control. After all, five hundred tons of locomotive and rolling stock requires some considerable distance to come to a standstill.

As the train rapidly decelerated Rob moved to the door, and dropped the window. He waited until the train came to a complete stop, then leaned out, grabbed the handle, and opened the door. He dropped to the ballast below, and was immediately into a run. He was down the embankment, over the fence, and running across a field in no time at all. How he wished that he had been wearing his trainers.

With the lactic acid building up in his leg muscles to a point where he couldn't stand it any longer, and his chest heaving, as he gasped for oxygen, Rob slowed his run to a gentle jog. He could see houses in the distance. *Somewhere to hide whilst I make my plans; somewhere to get food and drink,* he thought.

But at no time whilst making his plans did Rob think about working for a living. He was a chancer, with absolutely no respect for authority. He smiled once again as he walked with a swagger into the outskirts of London.

THIRTEEN

A Way of Life

Sam Forbes had known no other life. He was born on a boat, had grown up with boats, and was now a Number One; he owned his own boat. His earliest memories were of the old horse Billy, which pulled his parent's boat, Windrush. He had walked miles leading that horse, before he was big enough to help steer, or work the locks.

Before he was ten, he had been lent to his Uncle Albert and Aunt May, to help them out. It had been a wrench, but that was the way of the Boat People.

He was eighteen when he first spoke with Rachel in a serious way. They were married two years later, and bought a boat and horse. They had one child, a son they named Samuel, after his father. The birth had not gone well, and they were told that there would be no more children. They were content with life, however. The boy was strong and healthy, and as he grew they made plans to buy a second boat. With the new boat 'Phoenix' powered by a single cylinder diesel engine, there was power enough to pull the old boat fully laden behind. With loads of fifty tons or more, there would be enough money to support the three of them. Life was good.

But the Germans had other ideas. Young Samuel answered Lord Kitchener's call, and waved them a cheery farewell. That was the last time they saw him. When they got the telegram, Rachel's life effectively ended. She never recovered from the deep depression that set in, and died, some say of a broken heart, within two years. Sam sold Windrush, and worked Phoenix single handed. It was hard work, but he had little choice.

It was whilst carrying a full load of coal that Sam and the Phoenix approached Newton Magna locks. As the front of the boat slid almost silently into the bridge hole, that led to the lock gates, Jack noticed the name Phoenix painted on the bow.

The engine note then picked up, and there was a boiling effect in the water as the steerer put the engine into reverse. The boat stopped, just touching the lock gates. The engine was once again put into forward gear, and a very slow thump, thump sound emerged, as it was left on tick over, to hold it in position.

"Morning young'un," Sam Forbes said as he stepped from the boat.

"Morning," was all that Jack could think to reply at that moment.

"Well make yourself useful, and get them paddles up. Time's money."

It was as though Sam had spoken a different language, Jack just stood there open mouthed.

"Haven't you ever worked a lock before?" Sam said, as he took an angled metal key from his belt. Jack was to find out later that it was called a Windlass.

"Better show you what's what then. The least you can do is help me with the gates."

Jack was still silent, as he watched Sam run up the steps to the lock gates that were holding back the boat. Sam fastened the windlass onto a spindle, and wound a ratchet device that lifted from its support post. Outside the lock, the water boiled as somewhere below the surface the paddle opened, and water from above the gates rushed out. Now Jack realized why the boat had been left in forward gear. It was keeping it in position, despite the rush of water. Whilst Jack stood there transfixed, Sam literally sprang onto the balance beam and hurried across the top of the lock gates. Within seconds, he had wound up the paddle on the far side. The lock was empty in no time, and the boat pushed open the gates. It then crept along the lock, with barely any room to spare, and came to rest against the top gate. Sam by this time was closing the gates behind the boat. He dropped the paddles on those gates, shot up to the top gate, and wound up the paddles on that one. Slowly at first, and then as quickly as he could.

The boat rose rapidly, as the lock filled with water. With the engine still in forward gear the boat was gently pressing against the top gate. There was no need to wait to open the gate. The boat pushed it open as soon as the water level inside the lock equalled that above it. As the boat emerged, Sam stepped back onto his boat, gave a cheery wave and was on his way. It had taken him very little time to negotiate the lock, and Jack couldn't but marvel at his expertise. Jack was determined to help, in any way that he could, at the next lock.

"All right if I give you a hand?" He shouted over the noise of the diesel engine.

"Always glad of some help," Sam shouted back.

Jack ran along the towpath to the next lock, and helped Sam to the best of his ability. By the fourth and final lock, Jack was beginning to understand how everything worked.

And as Sam and the Phoenix left that last lock at Newton Magna, it dawned on Jack that here was perhaps the opportunity he needed.

"I don't suppose you need some help with the boat Mister?" Jack shouted. Sam adjusted the engine speed to idle, and was then easily able to converse with Jack as they travelled along the canal at walking pace, Sam on the Phoenix and Jack on the tow path.

"Sam's the name."

"Jack, Jack Bussey." There was no reason not to use his own name. No one would be looking for him, how could they be? But having blurted out what he had, he was stuck with it. From now on he would be Jack Bussey.

"Looking for work lad?"

"Work, and lodgings."

"What about your family?"

"My parents are no longer alive," Jack said. It was the truth after all, as neither had yet been born.

"Bit of a fix then?"

"Yes."

"Jump on at the next bridge lad."

Jack hurried forward, and waited for the Phoenix under the next bridge, where the towpath protruded, and the canal narrowed. He stepped onto the boat, as the rear end drew level.

"Better stand on the side Jack, or I might sweep you off with the tiller." Jack assumed that must be the name for the long metal handle that Sam was using to steer the boat. It was obviously a working boat. There appeared to be very little space for living quarters. No doubt he'd get a closer look later.

The steady thump, thump, thump of the engine had a semi hypnotic effect. With each beat the exhaust shot from the tall pipe on the top of the engine room. But not straight up like that of a steam locomotive. On the very top of the exhaust pipe was a polished brass ring, which split the gases in two, sending them sideways.

"Why the ring on the exhaust Sam?" Jack eventually asked.

"It disperses the fumes. Stops me choking, especially in tunnels," Sam replied.

The next thing that Jack noticed was a small hatch on the roof of the engine compartment. He could work out the purpose of that for himself.

The canal followed the contours of the English countryside, winding this way and that. It seemed to take an eternity to travel any significant distance. Jack decided to try an experiment. He picked out an object on a nearby hill, and tried to judge how long it would take before he would lose sight of it.

"How fast do you travel Sam?" Jack asked, after his last chosen landmark disappeared from view.

"'bout four miles an hour. Depends on the water."

"How's that?"

"Well, if the water's shallow we can't go so fast. And if we go too fast we'll wash away the banks."

"But it must take a long time to get anywhere?"

"In a hurry lad?"

"Well, no."

"No problem then, is it?"

"But what about the loads you're delivering? They must have to wait days for them to arrive"

"Only for the first load."

"I don't follow you," Jack said, lowering his eyebrows, as if in deep thought.

"Well say you want twenty ton of coal delivering every day; you send the first boat off with twenty ton. The next day another boat starts off with another twenty ton. And every day after that, a boat starts off. Now if the journey takes three days, how long will it take for the coal to arrive after the first boat gets there?"

"A day."

"That's right Jack. It's just a matter of good planning."

"But why the winding route?"

"Kept down the price of building the cut. Didn't need too many locks, cuttings, embankments, or worst of all, tunnels. Besides, locks use a lot of water. Can't flow back up hill can it?"

"It can if you pump it up."

"Perhaps they'll do that one day then Jack."

Jack realized that he would have to be careful. He didn't want to appear too clever, or come up with too many ideas. After all, if he tampered with the past, he could well affect the future. At this particular time, however, he didn't know in which direction his future lay. He decided that it would be a good idea to keep quiet, and to just observe.

He watched Sam pushing the tiller bar one way, and then the other. The boat responded to every movement. When Sam pushed it to the right, the boat would turn to the left, and when he pushed it to the left, it would turn to the right.

He watched Sam slow the engine, by means of a brass wheel, when approaching bridge holes. These were places where the canal narrowed as it passed beneath bridges. Some were very sharply curved, with intricate spiralled brick work, and the view was somewhat restricted. They prompted another question.

"Why such narrow bridges Sam?"

"What did I say about cost Jack?"

"You mean, the smaller the bridge, the less it cost?"

"Exactly."

"They weren't daft, were they?"

"Far from it lad. They only had so much money, and couldn't afford to waste a penny."

That was another thing that Jack would have to get used to, the money in the nineteen thirties.

Everything Sam did was smooth and unhurried, the mark of a man at one with his environment. And without the noise of road traffic, Jack was becoming used to the sound of the boat's engine. It was almost like a steady, strong heartbeat. And Jack was beginning to feel the presence of nature all about him. That was certainly something he had never really noticed before. There was the sound of birds singing. The sound of pigeons in the trees.

And as the light began to fade he saw the low soundless flight of a barn owl in a nearby field. The early evening had a smell all of it's own, and Jack felt more relaxed than he had done for a very long time.

By now the light was failing fast, and Sam was having to concentrate hard. "Just round this next bend," he said as he pushed the tiller to the left, and the bow began to turn to the right. Jack couldn't help but admire the ease with which Sam was steering such a long boat on a twisting canal. On a number of occasions Jack thought the bow would strike the far bank, but it never did.

As he looked around in the gloom, Jack could just make out the shape of a church spire. It must have been visible to Sam for some time, but Jack had only just noticed it.

"Where's that?" Jack asked.

"That's Braunston Church," Sam said. "Won't be long."

As they negotiated a left hand bend, Jack saw ahead, on his right, two bridges where the canal allowed turns from either direction.

"That's where you turn to travel north on the Main Line, and south on the Oxford," Sam said.

"But how can one canal go north whilst the other goes south, when it's the same bit of water?"

"Think of it as an X Jack, where both the left parts go in

one direction, and the right parts in another. Where they're together for a while they travel in opposite directions."

"I'll take your word for that." Jack couldn't quite grasp the concept. It would become a lot clearer later, when he travelled over that section of canal.

Sam slowed the engine, and as before, gently brought the boat to a stop, this time a matter of inches from the edge of the canal for mooring. There were metal rings set in the concrete, and Sam quickly tied up the boat, and stopped the engine.

"No need to cook today," Sam said.

"Jack's heart sank.

"The Old Plough's got the best grub around here."

"But I've no money for food," Jack explained.

"No bother lad, I'll pay. You can work for it over the next few days."

A smile settled on Jack's lips. At least he could eat, *and how hard could the work be?*

"Bit of a walk now Jack, but it'll be worth it."

Sam was right, it was a 'bit of a walk'. They walked over a bridge, then up a lane that climbed steeply to the village of Braunston. The village straddled the top of the ridge above the canal. Jack was to find out later that the railway station sat on the other side of the valley, a short distance from the canal.

The Old Plough was warm and welcoming. The bar was filled with other boat people enjoying a drink, and chatting noisily. At the far end of the room a couple sat, the husband with a pint mug in his hand, his wife with a red coloured drink in a round stemmed glass. Next to them sat another couple, with similar drinks, who were possibly members of the same family. The atmosphere was very thick, and Jack noticed that nearly every man was smoking, mostly cigarettes but some had pipes. Simple pleasures in a simple time. He certainly wasn't about to enlighten them about the dangers involved.

Then somebody started playing a small accordion, the type that Jack had seen played by sailors in old films. Within seconds the chatter had turned to singing. It was rough and ready, but everyone seemed happy. The atmosphere was intoxicating, and Jack's mind drifted.

He was brought back to reality by Sam.

"Come on Jack, eat up."

Jack hadn't even noticed that the food had arrived.

***

Sam was right, the food was good. The meat pie and potatoes filled Jack's empty belly, and the glass of cider gave him a comfortable feeling.

"Who's the lad then Sam?" A broad built man enquired.

"My new crew," Sam replied.

"Where did you find him?"

"Newton bottom lock."

"Looks fit enough."

"He will be," Sam replied.

Jack picked up on those words. *He will be,* he thought. It sounded as though he was in for some hard work. But then survival was the aim. If the work was going to be hard, so be it.

***

The question of just where Jack was going to sleep hadn't occurred to him. But as they left the Old Plough, and made their way back to the boat, the mental picture of the boat caused Jack a few anxious moments. Sam had seen the look on Jack's face.

"Don't worry son, you've got your own bed."

Jack was still uneasy. After all, he didn't know Sam, and here he was, about to share a room no bigger than the smallest room in his house, but with a roof that was considerably lower.

Jack hadn't realized just how dark it can get when you' re away from a built up area. Even in his home village of Newton Magna, there was always a bloom in the night air from the street lights. Here in the countryside, away from the highly efficient street lights of the modern age, the blackness made the world close and intimate.

"Now careful Jack, don't want you taking a look."

"A look at what?"

"The cut. Don't want you falling in the cut."

"You're not the only one Sam."

"Just wait there a moment Jack, and I'll open up, and light the lantern."

Sam stepped onto the boat, opened the rear doors, and after a few moments the cabin lit up, as he adjusted the flame.

"OK Jack, in you come."

Jack stepped carefully from the towpath to the boat. In the soft light from the lamp, he could now see the splendour of the cabin, and appreciate the use of the space.

"It's like the Tardis," Jack said.

"The what?"

"The........" Jack suddenly realized that Sam had never heard of Dr Who. "Oh, it's just a name for somewhere that's bigger on the inside than it looks from the outside," he said quickly.

As soon as Jack entered the cabin, he appreciated how 'house proud' Sam must be. There was a place for everything, and everything was in its place. Cooking and heating was taken care of by a miniature range immediately to the left. The flue pipe passed through the roof to the left of the hatchway. The range was black leaded, and immaculate. The heat radiated from it, and would keep the steerer warm in all weathers. Opposite to the range was a seat that ran the length of the cabin. Beyond the range, on the left, there were lockers, cupboards and drawers. And across the boat, at the far end, was the bed that could be shut away during the working day. The table was the front of a cupboard let down. Just inside, and to the left of the hatchway, were three large highly polished brass knobs. These reflected the light from the lantern, and Jack surmised that they were for decorative purposes.

Sam made them each a cup of cocoa, and they sat talking.

"Have you always worked on the boats Sam?"

"Never done anything else."

"And how old were you when you started?"

"I suppose you could say I started before I was born. You see the family's always worked on the cut. I was born on a boat, and lived on one ever since."

"But wouldn't it be better to work the boat two handed?"

Sam took a deep breath before telling Jack about losing his wife and son.

"I'm sorry Sam," Jack said. "I didn't know."

"No way you could lad. Not to worry; got to keep moving forward. Like the boat really; if you don't keep moving on you'll go under."

Jack thought about his own family. They were effectively lost to him. But he could not imagine how Sam must have felt losing first his son, and then his wife. Jack would have talked all night if Sam had let him. It was Sam that called it a night.

"Time for bed Jack, early start in the morning."

Jack had forgotten about the problem of sleeping arrangements. Sam opened the rear doors and slid back the hatch.

"Where you going Sam?" Jack asked.

"As I said Jack, time for bed."

"But where are you going?"

"Didn't think we were sharing did you?" Sam said, a wide grin on his face.

"The thought did cross my mind."

"No Jack. Didn't think the engine was that big did you?"

"Never thought about it."

"I've had an extra bed cabin built on the boat, ready for when I found a trainee mate like you. Doesn't cost me much cargo space. Come on lad, I'll show you your bed."

Immediately ahead of the engine room was a slim

compartment, with just enough room for a bed. Sam lit the lamp, and stood back.

“Good night then Sam, and thank you.”

“Good night Jack.”

Sam slid the hatch shut and closed the door behind him. Jack turned down the lamp, and settled into bed. He was asleep in moments.

FOURTEEN

Capital Ideas

Rob's first day away from his home county had been somewhat different to Sam's. He had wandered the streets somewhat aimlessly, looking for an opportunity to come his way. And as he walked passed various shops, he spotted a notice in one of the windows: –

VACANCY FOR SHOP ASSISTANT
– APPLY – WITHIN

No chance, thought Rob, *you won't catch me working in a shop.* Cash *and food – food and cash,* the words went round and round in his mind. As for food, there was no chance of a Big Mac or KFC. Fish and chips would be the nearest he could get to what he thought of as real food. Of course rob hadn't a clue about money in the 1930s, but he'd work it out soon enough. All he needed was the right opportunity. It came his way twenty minutes later, as he was trying back doors on a row of terraced houses. It came as such a surprise to him when he found a door that was unlocked, that he nearly fell into the kitchen. The door slammed back against the wall, making the saucepans on a nearby shelf rattle. Rob froze, and listened. All was quiet.

The house was a two up two down terraced, modestly furnished. Moving quickly from room to room Rob checked the various drawers and cupboards. Ten minutes later he was pulling up a chair in a nearby cafe.

A young waitress came over.

"I'll have pie and chips, and two slices of bread and butter," Rob said before she could speak. "And I'll have a large coffee," he added.

"Was there anything else?" The waitress said, *like manners,* she thought.

"No, that's it."

Rob had found some cash in a tin in the back bedroom of the house, and was now busy trying to work out the notes and coins. He had pound notes, ten shilling notes, silver coins of various denominations, and numerous copper coins. He found the size and weight of the penny coin to be somewhat out of proportion to its value. What he didn't appreciate was just how valuable the haul had been to its rightful owner. *Imagine having a hundred of these,* he thought whilst studying the penny; not realizing that two hundred and forty were required to make a pound in 1930.

***

With a full belly, and a lighter pocket, Rob headed further into the bustling Metropolis.

Sitting down on a low brick wall, he eased off his boots, and flexed his toes. *These boots have got to go,* he thought. *And I could do with smarter gear.* He couldn't help but laugh out loud when it dawned on him that store security in the 1930s would be nothing like that of the twenty first century.

By the time he had visited a number of shops, and department stores, Rob's appearance had changed completely. Now when he checked out his reflection in a shop window, he was pleased with what he saw. It wasn't what he would call trendy, but it was stylish in 1930. And he had no intention of spending another uncomfortable night. But if he was going to find somewhere acceptable he would need to ensure that he had enough money. *What a shame they don't have cash points in 1930,* he thought.

FIFTEEN

The Second Call In

Paul and Carol Fletcher was spending their second night without their son. Paul was physically exhausted from taking part in the search. Carol was mentally drained.

"They'll find them love. Two thirteen year olds can't just disappear," Paul Fletcher said, as he brought his wife yet another cup of tea.

"But where, and in what condition?"

"You mustn't think like that. We've got to stay positive."

"I know, but it's hard. He's never gone before. Why should he have run away now?"

"I don't know, but we'll find out when he gets back."

Carol Fletcher jumped when the doorbell rang. It was Toby Morton.

"Sorry to call so late," he said. "But I thought that you would like an update."

"We appreciate that," Paul Fletcher said, as he invited the officer into the house.

"We've completed the physical search of the area, and as expected, we've found no sign of the boys. That's got to be good news. I mean, no one's going to be able to take two thirteen year old boys away without a problem. And we've no reason to believe that any harm has come to them."

"Thank you Toby. It's very good of you to come. You must be exhausted," Paul said, as the officer made to leave.

"There'll be plenty of time to sleep when the job is done. I'll keep you informed of every development."

"Thank you," they both said, as Toby turned and stepped outside. They watched him drive into the distance, and then closed the front door.

"Come on love, let's get some sleep," Paul said.

It was a long restless night.

SIXTEEN

Early Start

Jack was fast asleep when Sam swung back the door, and pushed the hatch forward.

"Time to get up Jack lad."

Back in the rear cabin, Sam lit a small primus stove, in order to make some tea. Then he cleared and relit the range in order to start breakfast. The tea was good, and the porridge was hot and filling.

As they cleared away, a pair of working boats passed them travelling in the opposite direction.

"Good time to move Jack, we'll have a good road ahead of us."

"A good road?"

"Yes, with those boats coming the other way, the locks will be set for us."

It occurred to Jack that, if the water was at the same level as the boat approaching each time they came to a lock, then considerable time would be saved. If the level was wrong, it would mean emptying or filling a lock each time before they could use it. That would be wasteful of time and water. He rightfully presumed that finding the canal in that condition would be termed having a bad road. If he paid attention, he would soon pick up the language of the boat people.

The engine room was as well kept as the cabin. The engine was spotlessly clean, and the copper and brass work was highly polished. Sam showed Jack how to start it up. There was no simple turning of an ignition key. There was a strict procedure to be followed, which included heating, priming, and a good deal of patience and leg muscle power. Jack was an enthusiastic pupil, but he had his doubts as to whether or not he would be able to start the engine unaided.

As they left Braunston, heading south, Jack marvelled at the activity all around. There were men in boatyards, busy building and repairing boats. Working boats, some in pairs, lined the canal. There were empty boats where washing hung on lines strung over the holds. Women were washing and cleaning their boats. Brasses were being polished, and ropes scrubbed white.

Then suddenly before them, just passed a bridge was the first of the six locks that lifted the canal over thirty five feet to the summit level. At the third lock Jack noticed that there was yet another pub.

With the locks behind them, Jack stepped back onto the boat. He had only been on board a few moments when they entered Braunston tunnel. This was a new experience for Jack. It took a while for his eyes to adjust to the dark. The headlight on Phoenix showed the curve of the tunnel roof. Jack wanted to ask questions, but the sound of the exhaust from the single cylinder Bolinder engine was almost deafening, and prevented any conversation between them.

They had been travelling for a while when Jack saw the headlamp of a boat travelling in the opposite direction. It seemed impossible for two boats to pass in the confined space. The closer they became, the more worried Jack became. Sam eased the power, and the engine note slowed to a steady thump.................thump. Jack was relieved when the bows passed each other without contact. As the stern of the oncoming boat passed, Jack saw that there was another boat tied closely to the back of the motor boat. In the restricted light of the headlamp, he saw the figure of a woman, standing at the rear of the second boat, right arm resting on a large, curved, wooden tiller bar. Sam exchanged greetings with both steerers. In Jack's time people hardly spoke. In this time everyone seemed friendly.

Phoenix emerged from the confines of the tunnel, into a tree lined section of canal that was bathed in early morning sunshine. At last Jack could talk again with his companion.

"Right Jack," Sam said suddenly. "Time you had a go at steering."

Jack had to admit that he was apprehensive. But he was also excited, and felt honoured to be given such responsibility.

Sam moved over, allowing Jack to slip into position for steering. Being tall for his age Jack had a good view, as he took the tiller with his right hand.

"Now don't worry," said Sam. "I'll work the controls when necessary."

Prior to the handover Sam had slowed the engine slightly, to make it easier for Jack to steer. Jack had studied Sam's technique, and soon began to feel comfortable. Although it must be said, Sam had very sensibly chosen a relatively straight section of the canal for Jack's baptism.

As they approached a bridge, Sam took over, and Jack realized there must be hazards ahead. He had enjoyed steering, and was looking forward to his next lesson.

They passed under the bridge, and Jack could see that the canal turned to the right, where there was a wharf. Immediately to the left, after the bridge, was a tiny cottage, before the canal branched off.

"That's the Leicester Line Jack. Takes you all the way to the Trent."

"And have you been that way Sam?"

"I have, but not often. And not for some time."

The conversation was cut short, as they approached the top lock of the Buckby flight. The locks were set in their favour, and Jack stepped off the boat as it slid into the lock chamber. Immediately to the right was yet another pub, that was well positioned for both canal and road traffic.

"There are seven locks Jack, so you might as well stay on the towpath, and set them. No point jumping on and off."

It made good sense to Jack.

It was as Jack was half running to the second lock that he encountered his first horse drawn boat. There was of course no warning of its approach. No thump of an engine. A man, probably in his sixties, was leading what looked like a mule.

"How do you do young'un?" The man said.

"Morning," Jack responded, as he carefully made his way passed.

From the mule, Jack saw that a long rope stretched to the boat, which glided along almost noiselessly. Leaning on a large curved wooden tiller, like the one on the second boat in the tunnel, was a stoutly built woman, no doubt the man's wife. Jack thought how peaceful the travelling would be, but perhaps also how lonely. After all there would be little conversation between husband and wife. Jack would have a number of questions to ask Sam, when he re–joined the Phoenix.

They worked through the locks quite quickly. With the horse boat travelling in the opposite direction, all the locks had been set ready for them. *Another good road,* Jack thought.

***

"Horse boats Sam, what happens when you meet one?"

"Well, first of all, you always give them priority. After all they can't manoeuvre as easy as we can."

"But what do you do about the rope?"

"Nothing, that's down to the man leading the horse boat. It's up to him to lift the rope over your boat. But that only happens if the towpath is on his left of course. Got to keep your wits about you though. If he gets it wrong, you could lose some of the stuff on your roof. Many a good water can has been lost that way. That reminds me of something I wanted to tell you. You know the buildings near the top lock we've just gone through?"

"Yes."

"Well that's where you can get a highly decorated water can, like the one we've got here on the top of the boat. It's called a Buckby Can, after the place you gets it from."

Jack had noticed that most of the boats he had seen had such cans.

As they continued their journey south, Sam gave Jack instruction on the engine controls, and allowed him to steer for progressively longer periods. Sam must have felt confident; he gave Jack control as they approached Blisworth Tunnel. Jack accepted, but he wasn't as confident as his mate.

The tunnel was long, and several boats passed them in the opposite direction. Each time one approached, Jack slowed the engine.

By the time they emerged from the gloom of the tunnel into the bright daylight, Jack was no longer nervous. He had steered a loaded working boat, over twenty metres in length, through a tunnel, the best part of three kilometres long. And he had also safely negotiated the hazards of boats coming in the opposite direction.

"Well done Jack. Now it's time to exercise those legs of yours."

"More locks?"

"More locks."

They travelled round a left hand bend, and there before them was Stoke Bruerne, a virtual hive of activity. To the left a three–storey building dominated the scene. At the far end of the building there were a number of cottages. On the right, The Boat public house, and all around boats with their attendant crews. Directly ahead lay the top lock, and Jack could see a boat rising in the chamber.

"That's a bit of luck Sam, another good road ahead."

"Getting the hang of this, aren't you?" Sam said.

Jack kept thinking about the long tunnel that they had passed through, and found that he had another question for Sam.

"Sam."

"Yes Jack."

"I've been thinking about the horse boats, and the tunnel."

"Bit of a problem that, hey?"

"Go on then Sam, tell me how they get the boat through the tunnel."

"Well with only two people on the boat there's a bit of a problem. So they pay 'leggers' to take the boat through whilst they lead the horse over the hill."

"And what do the 'leggers' do?"

"They put boards on the boat, on each side, lay on the boards with their heads together, and take the boat through by walking along the tunnel sides."

"That sounds like hard work."

"It is, but that's how they earn a living."

"What happens if a boat comes the other way?"

"They have to pull in the boards, and start again when they have passed."

"That must take some time."

"Some time, and a lot of effort."

As the hours passed, Jack became proficient at working the locks. Although it would be some time before his muscles grew, and his strength improved.

Sam was surprised at just how quickly Jack was learning the controls. *Hours of sitting in front of a computer screen had not been entirely wasted, after all.*

"You'll do very well on the boats Jack. I can hardly believe you've never been on one before."

***

They ate on the move, sharing the steering in order to allow each of them the chance to eat in comfort. It was a long, hard day, but Jack had enjoyed every minute of it. When he wasn't engaged in work he would take note of everything he saw. In particular, he studied the working practices of other boat people.

"I don't suppose you can travel any faster, can you Sam?"

"Not really, don't want to wash away the banks, or risk a crash at a bridge hole. You can do a lot of damage, even at slow speeds, when you weigh this much. Besides, if I try to go too fast, we'll end up travelling slower."

"How do you mean we'll travel slower if we try to go faster?"

"Well, it's like this. The cut is saucer shaped. There's

only so much water so you try to stay in the middle. If I were to increase the speed of the engine too much, the back of the boat would try to dig in, and the water wouldn't flow under us proper. So we end up slowing down and wasting fuel."

"Now I understand," Jack said. It was obvious that Sam knew all there was to know about boats and canals.

***

They moored up as the light faded, and enjoyed a hot meal on board that night.

"What do you think about the cut then Jack?"

""I like it Sam."

"Good, but you wait 'til the weather changes."

It was true; the weather had been kind so far. Working the boats all year round would be a totally different matter.

"What do you do when the canal freezes up Sam?" Jack asked.

"Depends how thick the ice is. We have ice breakers that keep the channel clear when they can. But sometimes it gets too thick even for them."

"Then what do you do?"

"Try to find a temporary job on the land. After all, I've got to live. Can't make money if the boat's not moving."

***

As Jack lay in bed that night he recalled all the events of the day. And he thought about the ice. In his day winters tended to be pretty mild. He had no idea what they were like in the twenties and thirties.

Although he was physically tired, Jack's mind was racing. It was the early hours of the morning before his body finally surrendered, and he fell into a deep dreamless sleep.

***

The next day followed the same pattern of working. There was a difference though in Jack's approach. He was more confident, and could therefore enjoy more of his surroundings, even when he was steering.

He'd never really taken the time to appreciate the countryside before. At fifty, sixty, or seventy miles per hour, travelling as a passenger in his father's car, he could only look into the distance. At three or four miles per hour, or less, he could watch the activities of the birds in the hedgerows that lined the canal. He even smiled to himself when an express passenger train roared passed, hauled by a gleaming steam locomotive. Jack's father was a steam railway enthusiast. What he would have given to see the sights that Jack was seeing.

It was as they were travelling along a lock free stretch of the canal that Jack suddenly turned to speak to Sam.

"I was thinking," Jack said. "The canal through Newton Magna, well I wouldn't have thought that it was a very direct route to anywhere."

"Oh, you'd be surprised just how many places use canal carriers."

"But you said you picked up the coal at Atherstone,

and now we're here in London. Isn't there a more direct route?"

"I'll tell you something Jack; you're pretty smart."

"Why do you say that?"

"Because you're right, it's not the most direct route. I would usually travel down the Coventry Canal, the North Oxford, and then down the Main Line."

"Then why the change?"

"Collapsed bank Jack. It'll take them a few days to get it fixed."

"Couldn't you have waited?"

"No, that's something I can't afford to do."

"Don't you get paid? After all, it's not your fault."

"I'm what they call a number one, Jack. I own my own boat, I'm an independent. That means I have to find my own loads, and agree a price. I get paid for the job, a set amount. The quicker I can do it, the more I earn. So when there was a problem after I'd loaded, I had to make a decision. I either had to wait whilst they fixed the bank, which may have taken them longer than they thought, or go through Newton Magna, and only add a day and a half. You see it made more sense to go the long way round. Mind you, that route's not used much these days, and the locks are in a bad way. I reckon that cut will be gone in the next five years, if that."

"Oh, it won't, it'll last for years," Jack blurted out before he had time to think about what he was saying. He only knew the canal in his day, when pleasure craft used it regularly. He knew nothing of what happened in the intervening years.

“I wish I had your faith Jack, but the railways are taking a lot of the work away, canals won’t last for ever.”

Just wait until you see what they do to the railways, Jack thought.

SEVENTEEN

Ten Acre Farm

John Pollard had been in farming all his life. He was born on Ten Acre Farm, and when his father died, some two years after his mother, he became sole owner. It was the foot and mouth outbreak that had threatened his very existence. At one point he had been so desperate that he had considered suicide.

They say that it's an ill wind etc. etc. He had to admit that it was the widespread news coverage of the missing boys that had brought about the offer.

***

Wendy and Derek Coombs ran Newton Magna Post Office. Amongst Derek's many duties, was the role of postman to the village. He wasn't the fittest of men, and he was only too pleased that he rarely visited Ten Acre Farm, with its long steep approach.

He was sweating well by the time he reached the front door, that spring morning. The smell of bacon, just made matters worse.

"Morning John, got something for you."

"'nother bloody bill, I expect."

"Things that bad?"

"Don't come much worse."

"Is the kettle on then? I'm dying of thirst."

"Soon will be, I'm just 'aving breakfast."

"Smells good."

"It was."

***

Despite being a farmer, John Pollard was a private man. He waited until Derek had gone before he opened his letter. He didn't get a lot of mail, and always took his time when he did.

The letter was on quality paper, and had a fancy heading, which included contact details by either phone or Email. John skipped through this; he was eager to read the letter itself.

Dear Mr Pollard,

I represent Richard Graham Limited, Builders of Quality Houses.

We are looking to build a number of homes in the area of Newton Magna.

It is within our knowledge that you have considered selling all, or part of your land.

If you would like to find out more about our plans, and the huge financial benefits, please do not hesitate to contact me on the above telephone number.

Yours sincerely,

Michael Peterson.

Business Development Manager.

Richard Graham Limited.

A few years previously, the letter would have been in the bin before he had read the first few lines. This time the letter was refolded, and placed in the drawer, just in case.

EIGHTEEN

Clueless

It had now been several weeks since the boys had disappeared, and Sam and Jack had completed a number of trips together between London and Birmingham. They hadn't been on the Oxford Canal since that first journey together. It was only now that Sam had resumed his coal runs, and was travelling northwards for a load.

Back at Newton Magna the physical searches of the area had turned up no clues to the whereabouts of the boys whatsoever. Toby Morton was now systematically working through every contact the families had ever made. He worked non-stop, taking sleep whenever he could. He was a driven man. The dining room table was no longer a place to eat. It was buried beneath a mound of paperwork, which included maps, photographs, briefing papers, and various coloured pencils which Toby used to code his search patterns.

The kettle was in constant use, whenever he was at home. Black coffee tended to be the preferred drink. Even the numbers on the buttons of the telephone were showing signs of wear, his rough fingers having taken their toll.

***

John Pollard picked up the telephone, and then replaced it. He read the letter he had read so many times. *Why not?* He thought, *it's my land.*

"Good morning, Richard Graham Limited, Debbie speaking, how can I help you?"

John cleared his throat. He didn't like telephones, and very rarely used one. It was only in case he needed the vet for his beloved dairy herd that he had succumbed to the wretched thing.

"Ah, good morning, I've got a letter."

"Yes sir, can you give me the reference please?"

"Er, yes, just a moment."

"No problem sir."

"Er, here it is, reference RG137MP04."

"Thank you sir, I'll put you through to Mr Peterson."

There was a slight delay, during which he was treated to Beethoven's Fifth. He was just beginning to enjoy the musical interlude when it was suddenly cut off.

"Good morning Mr Pollard, Michael Peterson here."

"Yes, hello. It's about this letter you sent me."

"I've been looking forward to speaking with you Mr Pollard. Perhaps it would be advantageous if we met. How does Wednesday, two o'clock at Ten Acres sound?"

"Er, fine, yes."

"I'll see you then Mr Pollard."

Before he could reply, the phone had gone dead. *Wednesday it is then,* John thought.

NINETEEN

Friends Indeed

Stevie Banks had never known his father. Even his mother wasn't sure which of her visitors had left something behind. During the early months, his birth mother, Sandra Wright, had had a dilemma; whether to choose motherhood or booze. The booze had won. The result was inevitable; social services stepped in, and young Stevie started making the rounds. He'd lost count of the number of foster parents he had had. In the early days his stays had been lengthy. After all, most people like babies and toddlers. But as he grew older he became more of a 'handful', his behaviour and attitude leaving a lot to be desired.

Always a big lad for his age, he was now, at the age of seventeen, over six feet tall, broad, and with a face that only a mother could love. But not in his case unfortunately.

Stevie had lived by his wits for some time now, having run away from his last home, where he had been adopted, and given his surname. He was always on the make, always looking for an opportunity. Theft, burglary, and muggings had kept him fed and clothed, and somehow he had so far avoided arrest. In fact his lack of detention had built up his confidence to such an extent that he now believed himself untouchable. His plans of late had become more and more ambitious. Now he wanted the 'big money', and the high life that went with it.

***

The cafe was directly opposite the bank. Stevie had been planning the 'job' for weeks, and his notepad was full of encoded information. Opening times, pedestrian and customer footfall, security movement; every 'breath' that the bank took was recorded. He had worked out the how; now he just needed the when, and the who, for he was yet to recruit his team. Stevie had friends and associates, but it would be risky using them. Better to use new talent, with whom he had no ties. He would spend the next week putting the team together.

***

It was two days later, as Stevie was tucking into his full English breakfast, that Rob walked into the cafe. Stevie had seen Rob on a number of occasions, but they had never spoken. That was not about to change; well not at this location. It was too near the target. It was essential that no one witnessed any meetings between members of the 'gang'. He finished his breakfast, and ordered another mug of tea.

At his table Rob was tucking into a bacon sandwich. Twenty minutes later, he headed for the door. Stevie didn't move; not yet. He waited until Rob had walked away from the cafe. He downed the last of his tea, and stood up slowly.

By the time he left the premises, Rob was some distance ahead of him. There followed a game of cat and mouse, that lasted about twenty minutes, ending when Rob walked down a quiet side street.

"It's Rob, isn't it?"

Rob spun round.

"It's all right, don't worry, I'm not going to mug you," Stevie said.

Rob's heart was thumping, his mind racing. *Could I outrun him?* He thought.

"I've got a proposition for you," Stevie continued.

Might as well listen, Rob thought, whilst trying to calm himself down.

"Go on then," he said.

"Not here," Stevie said. "Do you know Andy's Cafe in Victoria Street? Be there at ten tomorrow morning, and I'll buy you breakfast."

"Is that it?"

"We'll talk while we're eating."

"Fair enough."

"Ten o'clock."

"Ten o'clock it is then."

Stevie turned, and rejoined the main road, leaving Rob wondering what this was all about.

***

Rob had been in the cafe for some time when Stevie arrived. He had deliberately chosen a table towards the rear of the premises, in a gloomy corner. Stevie ordered two large breakfasts, and pulled up a chair.

“I know what you do for a living,” Stevie said, before Rob could speak. “So don’t deny it.

“Who said I was going to,” Rob replied.

“How would you like to make more money in a day than you’ll thieve in a lifetime, doing it your way?”

Rob was taken aback, but he decided that he might as well listen to the proposition, especially as he hadn’t as yet got his free breakfast.

TWENTY

A Brief Encounter

Sam had known Ruth Smith since they were youngsters. The Smiths had worked a pair of boats for years. Ruth's dad Albert had kept his boats immaculate, and had ruled his family with a firm but fair hand. Ruth had been their only child, complications with the second one had seen to that.

Albert had been gassed in the Great War, and his breathing over the years had slowly deteriorated. When his wife Rose died in an accident, he decided that it was time to quit the boats and move onto the land. He and Ruth had worked the small farm ever since. Sam had kept in touch, as much as was possible, and over the years the friendship had blossomed.

It was as Sam and Jack were travelling north on the Oxford Canal one day that Jack met Ruth for the first time.

Sam suddenly slowed the engine and turned Phoenix

towards the bank. "Can't stop for long Jack, but I want to see Ruth, and pay my respects like."

There was nowhere to tie up properly. The bank was low and uneven, and the water was shallow. Sam ran the bow onto the mud, and turned the stern in. As soon as the back end found the bottom, he stopped the motor. He took a plank from the roof, and placed it between the boat and the bank. Then he ran across it quickly, before the boat moved, and took the rope. Having tied the ropes to two convenient trees, he gestured for Jack to join him.

Arhh, Jim lad, thought Jack. *Time to be walking the plank.* Well at least there was something at the end of it besides water.

The farm stood on a small hill, some distance from the canal, and Jack could see numerous dairy cattle grazing on the lush grass. Sam and Jack picked their way carefully between the cows and the fresh pats, until they reached the door of the farmhouse.

Ruth had seen them coming. The door opened, and there stood a woman about the same age as Sam. She had a kind round face, and rosy cheeks. Her hair was grey, and parted in the centre. It had then been wound into a bun on each side of her head, almost like a set of headphones.

Looks like Princess Leah from Star Wars, Jack thought. *Better not tell Sam that, won't have a clue what I'm on about.*

She was wearing a white apron over a green gingham dress. On her feet were stout, sensible shoes.

"Well I'll be blowed, Sam Forbes."

"Hello Ruth," Sam said as their eyes met, and there was a connection between them.

"And who's this young man then Sam?" She said, a broad smile on her face.

"Jack Bussey, Miss," Jack replied.

"At least he's got manners Sam. Not like some of them you know. Pleased to meet you Jack, and please call me Ruth."

"Can't stop," Said Sam; "Not this time. Just wanted to make sure you were Okay."

"I'm all right, but Dad's not so good. Don't reckon he'll last that much longer."

"Sorry to hear that," Sam said. "Anyway better go. Give my regards to your Dad, and we'll see you when we can."

"Don't know when that'll be," Ruth said. "Bye Jack, nice meeting you."

Sam and Jack returned to the Phoenix. And after Sam had poled the stern off the mud, he put the motor into reverse, swung the bow, and they were away again.

"Quick visit Sam," Jack said, as they left the farm behind.

"Not much chance to talk these days. Was better when she were on the boats. Then I'd get to have a good natter when we was moored up somewhere, loading or unloading. Sometimes we'd even get to have a drink in the Greyhound at Sutton Stop."

"Where's that?" Jack asked.

"Where the North Oxford meets the Coventry. We'll be there soon."

Jack could see boats tied up ahead, as they travelled round a long sweeping left hand bend. As the canal straightened, the lock came into view. Beyond the lock, on the left, were buildings, one of which, he found out later, was the Greyhound Pub.

"No need to get off Jack."

"Why's that?"

"You'll see."

The lock fascinated Jack. It only moved boats up and down about fifteen centimetres.

"What's the idea of that Sam?" He finally asked.

"Stops the other canal company pinching the water. Water means boats, and boats mean money."

After the lock, the canal made a ninety degree turn to the right, where it travelled under a bridge, and then joined the Coventry Canal, also at ninety degrees.

"Left for Coventry, right for Atherstone," Sam said.

It was a tight turn, but with the tiller hard over, and plenty of power, Phoenix swung round perfectly.

"Done that a few times, haven't you?" Jack said.

"Just a few," Sam replied.

They reached Atherstone late in the day, but they would have to wait until the following morning to be loaded.

TWENTY ONE

Clean Muck

The coal was delivered from above the boat, by way of a chute. In order to fill the boat safely it was necessary to move it along, until the required amount had been received. There were ropes hanging down for this purpose. It was a matter of pulling on the ropes to manoeuvre the boat into the correct position.

Having taken the load, Sam and Jack set about trimming it, so that the weight was correctly distributed in the boat's hold. The top planks were fitted into place, and then the boat was sheeted up. This was a matter of covering the load securely with different heavy tarpaulin sheets, which were then held down tightly by numerous ropes, or strings as the boatmen called them.

When the job was done, the boat, which now sat very low in the water, looked very impressive. The sides sloped in steeply, and there was a narrow flat surface at the top which would allow the crew members to travel from the back to the front of the boat.

The only trouble was, everything was covered in fine coal dust.

"Don't worry about that Jack," Sam said. "Coal's clean muck."

"How can you have clean muck?"

"I'll show you."

In no time at all the coal dust was brushed and swilled from the Phoenix. It didn't stick or stain.

"See what I mean Jack," Sam said, a satisfied smile on his face.

"Well, I've learned something today," Jack said.

"We all learn something every day Jack. You see, you never stop learning, that's what life's about. I never knew nobody who knew everything."

With the Phoenix ready to go, they had a quick cup of tea, and a bite to eat, before heading south. They had three days to make their delivery of coal. Three days to reach the Jam Factory.

***

Where the Phoenix had ridden high in the water, when travelling north, she now sat so low that 'the sparrows could drink from the gunwales', as Sam would say. The going was harder as a result. But at least the wind wasn't so much of a problem.

***

Towards the end of the first day, Jack was pleased to see the church spire of Braunston coming into view.

"The Old Plough Sam?" he said.

"Yes, I think we deserve a drink Jack, The Old Plough will do nicely."

The bar was as busy, and noisy as it had been on their last visit. But Jack now felt part of the boating community. He was earning his keep. If he never got back to his own time, he would certainly appreciate the work that his father was doing, instead of taking things for granted. In nineteen thirty, if you didn't work you didn't eat. It was as simple as that. There were no monetary handouts, like so many took, without giving anything in return, as he had heard his father say so many times.

Life on the canals was hard work, but it was uncomplicated. He saw no envy or greed, only friendship and mutual respect. How could things have changed so much in such a short time?

When Sam and Jack returned to the boat, Jack was in a talkative mood. "What do you know about the world away from the canals Sam?"

"Not a lot, but then I don't need to know a lot do I?"

"But wouldn't you like to know what's happening in other parts of the country, or even other parts of the world?"

"Not really. If it doesn't affect me then I'm not really bothered. Start worrying about things that don't concern you and you won't live long enough to enjoy the things that do."

Jack was about to tell Sam a few things he knew about

the outside world, but decided that silence was a wiser choice.

As Jack lay in his bed that night, he thought about what Sam had said. Perhaps his simple logic was the answer to the many stress related illnesses of his time.

TWENTY TWO

Withdrawal Symptoms

The day started well. Stevie Banks took out the car keys from his jacket pocket, and smiled. He'd had them for over five months, and now finally his patience was about to pay off. He'd done his research, and had found the house that he had been looking for. The occupants had been out, when he had entered from the rear. Searching the house methodically, Stevie had found the office diary, and a spare set of vehicle keys. Noting the details of various entries, he had slipped quietly away, leaving no trace of his visit.

Having checked the dates he had noted so long ago, he knew that no one would miss the car for some days; it was the perfect getaway vehicle.

Rob Bridges checked the time on his new wristwatch, and made his way towards the target area. He found the weight of the gun in his pocket reassuring. It was a Webley and Scott service revolver, .38 calibre. Stevie had acquired it on one of his night time excursions. The large house belonged to a retired army officer, who had no doubt kept the weapon as a souvenir of The Great War. Some distance away, and in separate locations, the remaining members of the team prepared for action.

Paul Morris finished his toast, and threw back the rest of his tea.

"Got to go luv," he said, as he leaned over, and gave his young wife a peck on the cheek.

"You take care," she responded.

Paul had joined the security firm fairly recently. He and Ruby wanted to start a family soon, and the steady, if modest, income would allow them to move their plans forward. They rented small but tidy rooms in an area that they believed would be suitable for bringing up children.

"See you later," he called as he pulled the front door shut behind him.

Ruby cleared the table, and gathered her things together. She was a linker at the local, family run hosiery firm. She checked her hands to ensure that there were no rough areas to snag on the stockings and socks she would be handling, and smiled a broad smile as she took yet another look at her wedding ring. She and Paul had been childhood sweethearts, and had married the previous year, after a long courtship.

Fred Cheney liked a good fry up to start off his day. He mopped up the egg with the last of his bread, and drained his tea mug. He lived alone, having lost his wife several years previously, after a long and painful illness. The small corner cafe was always his first port of call. After all, why cook when he could get a good, cheap breakfast locally, and avoid the washing up.

Paul and Fred met up at the security depot, and were assigned the bank run.

"Better stay alert today Paul," Fred said, grinning. "Some 'ard up sods out there might take a fancy to some of our money."

"It's not our money Fred."

"It is while we're in charge of it."

"Ever thought of just driving off with it?" Paul asked, whilst trying to keep a straight face.

"Now, let's 'ave none of them thoughts young man."

"Only joking; I'd never sleep at night if I ever did anything dishonest."

"I doubt that I'd get much sleep at night either with a young wife like yours."

"Hey, behave yourself."

With the van loaded, and the manifest complete, they waited for the outer doors to open.

***

The other two members of Stevie's team had never met. Yes, each member of the team had met Stevie, and had been briefed as to their respective roles in the operation, but their leader didn't want any friendships striking up, or any chance of careless talk being overheard. They would turn up at the agreed time and place, and each play their part. Stevie had used different locations for his recruiting, and briefings. The less each knew about the others, the better. Stuart Rawlings came from the north of the River, Richie Sullivan from the south.

At 10am. precisely, the security van pulled up outside the bank. And having checked that all was clear, Fred and Paul alighted from the vehicle, and opened the rear doors. Rob, Stuart, and Richie ran towards them from three different directions. Rob raised the revolver, and pointed it at Fred.

"Don't do anything stupid," Rob shouted, in as deep a voice as he could manage. The two security guards remained motionless, their hands raised. Stuart and Richie grabbed the money bags from the back of the van, and moved to the edge of the pavement.

Several members of the public were now watching from a distance. But one well-built man was striding across the road towards the scene, his eyes fixed on Rob. At that moment Stevie arrived, bringing the car to a sudden stop, the tyres squealing. Rob turned, and instantly saw the man approaching. He aimed the gun at the man's chest, and shouted.

"Stay where you are, I'll shoot."

"No you won't," the man replied, without breaking his stride. "You'll hang if you do."

The thought of hanging had never crossed Rob's mind. *1930's justice could be final.*

Stuart and Richie had by this time thrown the bags into the boot of Stevie's vehicle. But as they tried to open the side doors, the expressions on their faces changed; the doors were locked. At that instant two things happened. The big guy snatched the gun from Rob's hand, breaking

Rob's finger, which was on the trigger, and Stevie hit the accelerator pedal hard.

"So long chumps," he said out loud, as he sped away from the scene, and the guards, and members of the public, overpowered the three would be robbers.

By the time that Rob, and the others arrived at the police station, Stevie Banks was long gone. In fact no one would be looking for Stevie. As far as the other members were concerned their leader had been Ray Porter, Stevie had never revealed his real name. He had boarded the Carlisle bound express, clutching a rucksack full of cash, and with a single journey ticket he had purchased the previous day. And as he sat watching the countryside flash by, and the Royal Scot class locomotive got into its stride, he thought of home. After all, twelve months was a long time for a northern lad to spend in London, living under a false identity.

TWENTY THREE

Town and Country

Michael Peterson drove his immaculate Mercedes Sports car very carefully along the track to Ten Acre Farm. He pulled up outside the main building, opened the driver's door, and placed a plastic sack on the ground. He stepped gently onto the sack, reached into the back of his vehicle, and stood a pair of green Hunter Wellingtons on the plastic. He changed his footwear, and returned his handmade shoes to the car. Now resplendent in his mixture of city and country, the broad pin stripe of the blue suit contrasting vividly with the surroundings, he moved towards the door.

It was like interviewing a politician. John Pollard asked the questions, and Michael Peterson avoided answering them. His whole focus was on the amount of money that the farmer would come into.

"What the village needs is more housing, a new lease

of life. Built in such a way that it doesn't detract from the beauty of the area," Michael Peterson said.

"Well yes, I suppose more houses would be good. We certainly need to consider first time buyers."

"That's exactly right Mr Pollard, it's people wishing to buy a property in the village that we have in mind."

"I suppose we'll get to see the plans?"

"Of course, but don't worry, there's plenty of time for that."

"Just how much are we talking about?"

Peterson smiled, took the top off his expensive pen, and wrote on the back of a business card. He then turned it in order that John could see.

"That much?"

"Yes Mr Pollard, that much."

Peterson opened his brief case, removed some papers and placed them on the table. He turned to the last page.

"Just sign there Mr Pollard, I've marked the place with a cross."

"I've been thinking, perhaps I ought to 'ave someone look through the papers, make sure everything's right."

"No need for that John, may I call you John? By the way these biscuits are delicious. Now where was I? Oh yes, just a quick signature, I give you this very generous cheque, and we're all done."

"I suppose there's no point prolonging things."

John Pollard took the pen, and found the line for his signature. The door swung back with such force that the plates on the old Welsh dresser rattled, and threatened to fall.

"Quick John, there's a problem with Violet."

The look on young Jim's face told John Pollard that the matter was urgent.

"But your signature Mr Pollard," said Peterson, holding out his pen.

"Booger that, got to go. The old gel's one of my best milkers."

"But."

"No buts," John said, as he left his visitor alone at the kitchen table.

TWENTY FOUR

Big Ears

"Should have seen the look on his face when he didn't get his signature. Talk about disappointed. But my girls are more important than his commission."

Paul Fletcher looked up from his newspaper.

"Just how much has he offered you John?"

"Never you mind Joe Richards, that's my business."

"The money might be your business, but new houses concern everyone."

Paul folded his paper, slipped his reading glasses into their case, and moved to the bar.

"Yes sir, another pint?"

"Ah, yes please, and perhaps you'll join me?"

"Don't mind if I do." John Pollard's glass was emptied and back on the bar top in seconds.

"Very kind of you," said Joe, as he served the others. "I'll have a half with you."

It was the first time that Paul Fletcher had visited the pub since the boys had gone missing. In fact he had been there only a few times since he and his family had moved to the village, and he didn't want to appear pushy. It was a good hour later, after another couple of rounds of drinks at his expense that he broached the subject.

"Did I hear you say something about new houses?"

"It's this crafty old sod making a fortune, I'll be bound," Joe said, as he pulled yet another round of drinks. "Don't seem right really."

"Why's that?" Paul Fletcher asked.

"Well, I don't suppose they'd have heard of the place if it hadn't have been for……" Joe stopped mid–sentence. He was finding it hard going, and wished that he hadn't started as he had.

"For the boys going missing," Paul said.

"That's right, I'm sorry Mister Fletcher, didn't really like to say."

"That's all right Joe, not yours or anyone's fault. And if it does John some good, then I wish him all the best."

"That's very decent of you Mister Fletcher," John said, forcing a smile.

"After all, it's for the good of the Village isn't it. I mean, we could do with more houses, especially if they're right for first time buyers." Paul Fletcher was probing, hoping that he was right.

"That's what I heard him say," Joe said.

"Just how many are they intending to build?"

"Don't rightly know."

"But you've seen the plans?"

"Well, actually no."

"Hasn't anyone seen the proposals?"

"He told me that he had the Council's agreement, and everything was sorted."

"Have you got their details?"

John handed him Peterson's business card without thinking. Paul couldn't help but see the price on the reverse side, but said nothing about it.

"Would you do me a favour please John?" He said.

"What's that then?"

"Don't sign anything until I've looked into this. It seems a bit strange that he's got permission, and no one's seen the plans."

"All right then Mr Fletcher, I'll wait."

"Thank you John, and call me Paul."

They stayed together talking for some time.

***

"Good night gentlemen, take care."

Joe Richards closed the front door of the Bull's Head, slid the bolts into place, and turned the key in the lock. For his patrons this was the end of their evening. For Joe and his wife Kath, it was the start of phase two. It would be some considerable time before they could consider going to bed. The bar and lounge areas, which had been so alive and vibrant, were now like ghost towns. Chairs were pushed back; glasses, some with their contents only partially consumed, sat haphazardly on the tables. Empty crisp packets had been folded and tucked into empty glasses. One even sat in an inch of bitter shandy. At least these days there were no ash trays inside the pub. The environment was certainly a good deal healthier since the smoking ban.

"Is it all worth it Joe?"

It wasn't the first time that Kath Richards had asked that question.

"I mean, it's not much of a life is it at times?"

"Oh, I don't know," Joe replied. "We've good friends, and you do like it round here."

"Yes I do like it here, but I wonder how many friends we would have if we weren't supplying them with booze."

Joe leaned on the bar and asked, "Come on, what's the real problem?"

"Can't you guess?"

"We're doing okay, aren't we?"

"Not really Joe, I've been looking at the books again. Yes we have our regulars, and the occasional through trade, but quite honestly we're not moving forward."

"Any ideas?"

"Food, that's the answer."

"We do food."

"No not snacks, meals, proper meals."

"Yeah, well I can think of three major problems to start with."

"That's typical of you, always looking at the negatives."

"No, I'm just a realist."

"Go on then, tell me what these three things are."

"Space, finance, and customers."

"Hmm."

"If we could just think of something to bring in more people, we wouldn't need to think of anything special. After all bums on seats are what count. Increase the numbers, increase the turnover. Something will turn up." Joe said.

TWENTY FIVE

One Good Turn

It was more drink than Paul Fletcher had consumed in some time, and it took a while for his head to clear the next morning.

"How's the head?" Carol asked, as she poured the second cup of coffee.

"Not good."

"Serves you right, the state you were in last night."

"That's very nice. I'll have you know that I was drinking for the good of the village."

"That's got to be high on the list of excuses."

"No, it's true."

Paul told his wife about the conversation that he had had the previous evening, and the possible consequences if someone didn't act before it was too late.

***

It took Paul Fletcher several days to get an appointment with Michael Peterson.

"Now Mister Fletcher, what can I do for you?"

"I hear that you are looking to build in a village called Newton something, near to Market Clayton."

"And where did you hear this?"

"Oh, I have my sources. I'm in land acquisition and property development myself, and was wondering if there was an opportunity for me?" The first part of the statement was true.

"There could be. Where are you from Mr Fletcher?"

"I have a flat in London, but I'm looking to buy some property in the country, as an investment."

"Ah, then I could have something for you."

"Paul, please call me Paul, especially if we may do some business together."

There was a knock at the door, and Peterson's secretary came in, carrying a tray. She placed it down carefully on the side table.

"Thank you Debbie," Peterson said. "Help yourself to coffee and biscuits Paul, I'll just get the plans out."

Paul Fletcher moved to the table where the refreshments had been placed. The coffee pot, cups, plates, saucers, cream jug and sugar bowl were all matching fine bone china. There was a crest, and the name of the company on each item. The tray itself was solid silver, and also bore the company insignia. Paul poured himself a cup of coffee, and took a sip. It was obviously of the best quality. He smiled to himself as he took a biscuit.

Peterson swung back one of his framed certificates,

and opened the wall safe that had been hidden from view. He removed some papers, closed the safe, and finally, and carefully, repositioned the certificate. He lingered for a moment, no doubt reading the wording, and then turned to face his visitor.

"Can't be too careful these days," he said. "Never know who's going to pilfer one's ideas."

He spread the plans on his huge oak desk, and then poured himself a cup of coffee. Paul Fletcher could hardly believe his eyes, but his facial expression remained unchanged.

"Impressive, isn't it?" Peterson said, a smug smile on his face.

"Silly old sod doesn't realize what he's got. The views alone are worth a fortune."

"But how did you get planning permission, surely there had to be consultation. I'm presuming of course that there would be some local opposition?"

"It's surprising what you can do when you know the right people, and there's a local election coming up. They were only too happy to help. Said that the local economy would benefit. More likely that they would, Mr Graham can be very appreciative."

"But these are executive houses, I doubt if village people can afford them."

"I know that, and you know that Mr Fletcher, but as long as the village people don't get wind of it just yet, there won't be a problem. Now can I interest you in one of the plots, ideal for investment? Believe me, there'll be no shortage of takers."

As Paul Fletcher left the office the phone rang. It was Peterson's boss. He had been summonsed.

***

"Don't worry Mr Graham," Peterson said. "He'll still sign. John Pollard's not the sharpest knife in the drawer."

"Just make sure that he does." Richard Graham was in no mood for failure. He swung his high backed leather chair round, and faced the window. The meeting was obviously over. Peterson returned to his office and opened his diary.

TWENTY SIX

Silent and Deep

There was nothing unusual about seeing a police vehicle outside the Fletcher's house. Since the boys had gone missing, Toby Morton had been a regular visitor to both houses. On this occasion however, the subject did not involve the boys.

"Come in Toby, thanks for coming," Paul Fletcher said.

"No problem Mr Fletcher."

"No need to ask if you'd like a cup of tea Toby."

Toby smiled. He remembered what his first sergeant had told him when he joined the Force. "Never turn down the offer of a cuppa Toby, whether you want one or not. If you do, you might not get the offer on the next occasion when you're dying of thirst."

Paul Fletcher placed two large mugs of tea on the table, and sat himself down opposite his visitor. He took a sip of tea before speaking.

"You know about John Pollard being offered a large amount of money for part of his land?"

"I know he's had an offer, but I don't know how much."

"Let me tell you, it's a considerable amount."

"And how does that involve me then Mr Fletcher?"

"I believe that there is some corruption in the local council."

Toby's eyebrows lifted.

Paul Fletcher told the officer all that he knew to date. When he had finished, Toby took some time before responding.

"Looks like I'll need to do a bit of detective work. I'll need some help though."

"No problem Toby. I know a few people myself who could assist us."

They discussed, and refined their plan of action. Secrecy was all important. They would be making discreet enquiries, until it was time to blow the whistle.

TWENTY SEVEN

Old Betsy

Jack had been watching other boat crews working. He had noticed that many of the pairs of boats had crews of three. There would be one on the motor boat, one on the butty, and a third that would ride ahead, and set the locks. That way they seemed to move at a terrific pace. There were never any delays, or very few at any rate.

Jack brought up the subject one evening over supper.

"If I got a bike we could really get a move on, then you could earn some good money."

"We could."

"No Sam, it's your boat. As long as I can eat and have a roof over my head I'm all right."

"The next place we reach, you can look for a bike, and let's not have any nonsense about not taking your share."

"We'll see."

It was late when they reached Fenny Stratford, too late for Jack to look for a bike.

"What time will we start in the morning Sam?"

"Why, what were you planning Jack?"

"If I could manage to get a bike, it would be worth losing a bit of time tomorrow. We would more than make up for it over the following trips."

"Makes sense I suppose."

Jack was up early; even earlier than usual. Sam took the opportunity to work on the boat. But it was frustrating for such a hard worker as Sam to watch other boats passing. Every boater that passed made some comment.

Sam was relieved when Jack finally reappeared, riding an old black bike. Jack braked to a stop, swung his right leg back over the saddle, and stood proudly displaying his new found friend.

"Thought you'd at least get a man's bike Jack," Sam said.

"That's good. I get up early; walk miles; and all you can say is, I thought you'd get a man's bike."

"Sorry Jack, didn't mean to hurt your feelings."

"It was all I could get. And it only cost a few bob. Besides it will come in handy if you ever get a missus. I decided to call it Betsy. Betsy the bike."

"Yes, very nice. Now let's make up some of that lost time. Getting fed up of being shouted at by the others boaters. Have to keep telling the same story."

Jack swung Betsy on board and they were away as soon as Sam could start the engine.

TWENTY EIGHT

Jumping Jack

It was whilst Jack was on Betsy one day that she proved her worth. As Jack rode along the towpath he noticed that something wasn't right. He had passed the motor boat, heading in the opposite direction, and was just about to say how do you do to the woman on the butty.

She was obviously in great distress. Instead of leaning on the tiller staring ahead, all her attention was behind the boat. Totally reliant on her partner, over forty metres ahead, Rose Butcher had no way of turning back, or even stopping. Having just left his last lock, John Butcher had separated the boats, let out the long snubber rope in order to tow efficiently, and was accelerating away. The noise of the engine prevented any communication between husband and wife at that time.

Jack raised his hand in an attempt to attract the motor boat steerer's attention, but a cheery wave was all he got in return. It wasn't until he neared the butty that he learned the awful truth.

"My baby, my baby, he's in the water."

"Where?" shouted Jack.

"Under the bridge."

Jack looked along the canal. The bridge was a short distance ahead. He gripped the handlebars tight, and pushed down hard on the pedals. His heart was already beating fast. He would have only seconds if he was to succeed.

By the time that he reached the bridge hole his chest was thumping. The water was almost still, having recovered from the activity of the boats a few moments before. There was certainly no sign of the missing child. In one movement he threw the bike into the hedgerow, and leapt towards the water. He crossed his arms and his legs as he did, and was in the sitting position by the time that he hit the surface, thus minimising the depth of entry. Taking as deep a breath as was possible in the circumstances, he dived. He would get one chance, and one chance only. He was in luck. His right hand found something at the first attempt. It felt like an old sack. He heaved it to the surface, and found to his great relief that he had the two year old by his jacket.

Jack quickly cleared the boy's mouth. Then he gently held back his head, placed his mouth on the little face and carefully inflated the boy's lungs. There was no movement. He tried again, and there was a cough. Then another, and the boy spluttered into life. Jack stood in the water, the boy crying in his arms.

Rose Butcher had by now managed to attract her husband's attention. Her only option had been to steer the butty off course. The effect on the motor boat had been immediate, and John Butcher had turned to remonstrate with his partner.

It was a long, wet walk back for Jack, but he didn't care, the boy was safe in his arms. He reached the butty, as the Phoenix was approaching. Pushing the youngster into its mother's waiting arms, he turned to recover his abandoned bike.

"Hope you haven't lost that bloody bike," Sam shouted. "Look at the state of you!"

"Course not," was all that Jack could manage to reply. It was sometime later before Sam would learn the full facts; and not from Jack.

As they sat talking later, Jack turned to his friend.

"Do you believe in fate Sam?"

"Suppose I do a bit."

"But do you think your life's mapped out, and you can't alter it?"

Sam gave the question some thought before he answered.

After a few moments he said, "I think that we're given a sort of map Jack. And on that map, there's lots of choices. It depends on the choices we make, as to where we go, and how we get there."

Jack was somewhat taken aback by Sam's answer. There was more to his friend than he had realized.

"Do you think people can change?" Jack asked after a few moments.

“People can always change, it’s wanting to that really matters.”

Jack thought how good it would have been to have discussed the topic with his father. And as Sam sat quietly smoking his pipe, Jack thought back over the last few years of his life. If only he could get another go, to make things right, he thought.

TWENTY NINE

Building Friendships

Paul Fletcher hadn't visited Ten Acre Farm before, but he had met John Pollard on a number of occasions. When Paul had telephoned the night before, John had been curious as to what business he may have, but as usual had not asked. He was quite happy to delay that conversation until he was face to face. Phones were for emergencies, not for proper conversations, he always said. Far better to have a chat over a pot of tea than over a phone. No point rushing. After all, he could delay the person leaving, he couldn't stop them ending a phone call. Visitors were something special to be cherished.

***

"Come in Mr Fletcher, how are things?"

"Not bad John, not good, I doubt they ever will be. Just got to keep pushing forward. I tell myself that Jack, and Rob of course, have taken it on themselves to have an adventure. That way I can think more positively."

"Tea?"

"Please."

"Now what is it that's got you all worked up? I mean, I don't get many visitors out here on the farm. Too much muck I expect. Never bothered me."

"It's this offer you've had for your field."

"A good one, more than I ever expected."

"But do you know what they intend building?"

"Houses for first time buyers, that what he said."

"And what do you understand by that John?"

John poured the tea, and sat opposite Paul Fletcher at the old kitchen table.

"Like I said, houses for them in the village that needs to get in the housing market, so to speak."

"That's what they'd have you believe John."

"Well, what are they planning then?"

"They intend building a small number of large, executive houses for people who want to buy their first country property."

"You mean outsiders?"

"Exactly."

"Blow that for a game of soldiers. He can stick his money."

"And how would that leave you?"

"In a fix, but able to sleep at night. Couldn't do that to the village."

"I thought you'd say that. That's why I've got an alternative. Interested?"

"Always willing to listen."

THIRTY

A Break From Work

Sam looked up at the trees that stood on the far side of the canal. The tops were moving gently, but Sam could read the weather. High above, the few small clouds that were scattered haphazard across the sky, were moving faster than he would have liked.

"Better get going Jack, it's going to get rough later on."

"But what about breakfast?"

"We'll have it on the move."

Jack had to admit to himself that he was disappointed. He always enjoyed breakfast. It was usually porridge, but he had taken to it well. It warmed him through, and seemed to suit him. But it wasn't just eating, or drinking a large mug of hot sweet tea; something else he had taken to, it was the comradeship, and cosy feeling of the cabin of the Phoenix.

They made good progress, most of the locks being in

their favour, but the afternoon would be a different affair. By now, the sky was completely overcast, and becoming darker. The sound of the wind could be heard in the trees, despite the noise of the boat's engine. For a summer day, it was decidedly cold, and the odd large spot of rain was now falling, creating large bubbles on the surface of the water. If Jack had arrived on this day, he would have thought the climate had changed, as well as the date.

They passed a number of boats that were already tied up. Smoke was curling from their chimneys, their cabin doors closed against the wind. The wooden tillers on the buttys were curved upwards, signifying the premature end of work for the day. Jack envied them, but said nothing. What he did notice, was that they were all empty. None of them were carrying cargo. Sam answered Jack's question, before he could ask it.

"See how high they sit out of the water when they're not loaded. Get blown all over the cut, they do. We, on the other hand, being loaded down, can keep going a lot longer.

***

By the time that they neared Sam's intended mooring the sky was almost black, and it would only be a matter of time before the rain clouds released their heavy load. Jack pulled his cap well down, and stepped off at the bridge hole, taking the bike with him.

It was at that very moment, as he started along the already wet towpath, that the heavens opened. As he rode, head down towards the lock, the rain, driven by the wind, hit his face like cold needles. Under the wheels, the mud was clinging to the tyres, making the going even harder. Sam, well protected by the hatch of the Phoenix, screwed up his eyes against the now torrential rain.

Jack flung Betsy down, and began to set the lock, the first of three. He had the bottom gates open as the Phoenix appeared round the sharp bend.

As the deep lock swallowed the boat, Sam had a moment's respite from the weather. Jack closed the gates, and dropped the paddles, the boat pushing against the top gate. Then he raised the paddles before recovering the bike and heading for the second lock.

Had they followed the same system at the second lock there wouldn't have been a problem. But Sam wanted to speed things up. He wanted to tie up just passed the locks, and wait out the rest of the storm. After all, The Boat Inn did have good beer.

"I'll work this one, you get the last one ready," Sam shouted to Jack, as the bow slid into the lock chamber.

The third lock was round another bend, and some distance ahead. If it was ready, Sam would be able to go round the bend with a good deal of power on, which would help him against the wind. As Jack rode off, Sam climbed onto the roof of the cabin, scrambled up the lock ladder, and moved quickly to the gates. He dropped the paddle on the rear gate after closing it, held the wet rail and threw out his right foot to reach the far gate, which had half closed with the movement of the water.

The wind hit the gate with such force that even the

water couldn't hold it back. Sam's right foot slipped on the wet timbers, and he swung round toward the gate he had first crossed. The jolt was so violent that he lost his grip on the rail, and he fell from the gate, landing awkwardly on the rear of the boat. The pain was excruciating, and as hard as he tried he couldn't get to his feet.

The third lock had been ready for some time, and Jack had taken the opportunity to shelter in the doorway of the adjacent building. But his feeling of relief, at stepping out of the storm, turned to concern as the time passed, and the boat had not appeared. He turned his collar up, and climbed back onto his bike.

As he rounded the corner, he could see the top gate of the lock, but there was no sign of the Phoenix. It was not until he reached the lock that he saw the reason for the delay.

"Well don't just stand there, yer daft booger, get this boat out of here."

Jack closed the gate, filled the lock and stepped onto the boat.

"I've bust me bloody leg Jack, can't move at all."

"Have you hurt anything else?"

"Only my pride."

"I'll get you to the Boat Inn Sam, then we can get you fixed up."

Jack opened the door to the bar.

"Yes lad, what can I do for you?"

"It's Sam, Sam Forbes, he's broken his leg."

"Clumsy old sod, now how did he do that?"

"Fell off a lock gate."

"And where is he now then?"

"On the boat getting wet through."

"Better fetch him in here then."

It wasn't easy, but somehow Jack, and his new found friend Bill Sharpe managed to get Sam into the bar. Jack had strapped the tiller bar to his leg to immobilize it.

"Well that's that then Jack, no way I can work the Phoenix like this."

"Don't you worry about that Sam, let's get you sorted out first."

"I'll take you down the hospital Sam, missus will look after the pub," Bill added.

Bill Sharpe was a jolly individual, with a belly that suggested years of beer drinking. He was broad of back, with enormous hands. Jack was more than pleased with the help that he had found.

"Won't be too comfortable Sam, but can't see any other way of getting you there," Bill said, as he and Jack helped Sam into the back of the old van.

"It stinks in 'ere Bill, what you been up to?"

"Oh don't mind that Sam, it won't hurt you, never did my roses no harm."

By the time that they arrived at the hospital Sam wasn't feeling too good. He hadn't eaten since breakfast, and the feeling of hunger combined with the atmosphere in the old van had made him feel faint.

"When did you last eat Mr Forbes," the doctor asked as he examined the leg.

"Eight or ten hours ago."

"Just as well, going to have to knock you out to reset the leg."

"How long before I get back to my boat then?"

"Be a couple of days or so Mr Forbes, mustn't rush things. Of course you'll be in plaster for six weeks. That's if everything goes all right of course."

"But I can't afford not to work,"

"You can't afford not to get fixed up either, now can you?"

"Any chance of getting a light for my pipe?" Sam asked.

"Not in here, smoking is not allowed."

"I'll just have to suck the bloody thing then, won't I?"

***

Sam wasn't used to so much space, and the thought of sharing a room with strangers didn't suit him at all. The sooner he could get back to the Phoenix the better."

Jack stepped onto the boat, made himself some tea, and a sandwich, and sat thinking. *Why not?* He thought. Sam had done it before they met. Jack knew how to work the boat and the locks. Yes, why not in deed? He'd deliver the load on his own. It would be slow, hard work, but at least there would be some money, and Sam needed all the help he could get.

The storm was still raging, and Jack settled in. Outside it was cold, wet and windy. Inside it was warm and cosy. He would restart the journey at first light the next morning.

THIRTY ONE

Jack's Journey

Starting the engine was Jack's first problem. As he stood looking at the great inanimate object his mind went temporarily blank. Luckily his brain was only taking a breather. Jack had always been good at visualising things, and all he had to do was cast his mind back to when Sam had performed the operation.

Five minutes later, muscles aching, and brow dripping, the cold dead engine thundered into life. As long as it kept running then so would Jack. Two creatures working in harmony, one made of iron and brass, the other flesh and bone. Jack untied the ropes, and was on his way.

It was even harder work than Jack imagined it would be. It was fine whilst the canal was free of locks, but when he had to work them single handed, he found the going tough. What Sam had made look so easy, was extremely difficult. He realized that youthful enthusiasm was no substitute for years of practice, and the expertise thus gained. He managed somehow, but it was slow going. He made up his mind to never again judge anything without knowing all the facts.

It had certainly been a new and strange sensation for Jack. He had never before taken responsibility for anything. Now here he was, in sole charge of a working boat, capable of carrying tons of cargo. He was a working boatman, with great responsibilities. And for the first time, Jack felt part of the community. There was a camaraderie; friendship without imposition or obligation.

***

It took Jack hours to shovel out the coal. When he had eventually finished, he was black from head to foot, and completely exhausted. He would have loved to have just collapsed onto the bed, and fallen asleep, but he couldn't take dirt into the immaculately kept cabin. He cleaned himself up as best he could and took himself off to the office.

***

"Yes lad, what can I do for you?"

"Jack Bussey, off the Phoenix, looking for a load."

"Sam Forbes's boat the Phoenix, where's he got to then?"

"I'm his new crew Mr Herbert," Jack had read the name on the office door.

"Sent me to see about a load, whilst he gets the boat refuelled."

"I thought he was settled with the Jam Ole these days. But if he's looking for something I'll see what I can do. Come back in an hour and I'll have something for you."

"Thank you sir."

I like that lad, Ray Herbert thought, as Jack stepped from the office.

THIRTY TWO

An Hour To Kill

Jack knew that Sam regularly collected coal from Atherstone, and delivered it to Kearley and Tongues Jam Factory at Southall. But that involved travelling half the journey empty. If he could manage a load of any kind on the return trip he could make more money. He would have to clean out the boat of course, and that was no doubt the reason why Sam always carried coal. But some time cleaning could be offset against the extra income. It would need some planning, but then what else had he got to do?

Apart from the trip to the hospital, Jack hadn't left the canal since he had joined Sam on the Phoenix. Sam had given him a small amount of money to buy food, and here was the ideal opportunity to have a look around. It would be like stepping into yet another world. He had seen Newton Magna and Market Clayton wearing their nineteen thirties garb, but now here he was in London.

Jack left the boats behind, and walked through a gap to the streets beyond. It was fascinating to study the England of a lifetime ago; the people, clothes, and vehicles. The shops particularly held great interest for Jack. It was like a huge living museum, and entry was free.

As Jack wondered around a large department store, he completely forgot about the time. He had stopped looking at his bare wrist long ago. It had taken him sometime to break the habit. It's only when you are without a watch that you realize how many times you must look at it when you have one. Working on the boat, time didn't really matter, as long as you didn't waste any.

Jack remembered what someone had once told him. 'It doesn't matter who you are, or how rich or poor you may be, you will only receive twenty four hours each day. Spend those hours well, because you cannot get them back. There is no saving up time. All that has not been used properly is lost on the stroke of midnight, when a new twenty four hours is allotted. For the past is history, tomorrow a mystery. All we have is the gift of today. That is why they call it the present.'

Right now, Jack realized he had idled enough time away. He must return to the boat. It was as he stepped back onto the street that he got a severe shock.

Jack couldn't believe the change in the weather. He had known fogs, but not like this one. No doubt the Thames was playing it's part. It was the colour that worried Jack. It was yellowish, and irritated his eyes and throat. There was also a smell. It was the smell of smoke from hundreds of coal fires. *The yellow must be from the sulphur,* Jack thought. Perhaps not everything was better in nineteen thirty. He could only imagine what would happen to the surrounding countryside when rain was added to the London smog.

Jack wasn't panicking, but he was getting concerned. When he had left the boats, Jack had looked around as he walked. He was confident that he would recognize enough landmarks to be able to find his way back. But that was when the air was clear, and buildings in the distance added to the reference points. Now, with the smog swirling all around, none of these were available to him. There was no way that he could remember all the street names. If only he could find one name that he did recognize.

As the light was fading, Jack began to convince himself that he would never find his way. Then he saw it, at last a street name that he did remember.

By the time that Jack got back to the office, it was too late. The booking clerk was gone, and the door was locked. There would be no load on the return journey.

At least I won't have to clean the boat out, Jack thought. Just as well, he was too tired for anything. He was fast asleep the moment that his head hit the pillow.

THIRTY THREE

Two Day Dash

Jack had two days to get back to Braunston if he was to stay on schedule, and be able to pick up Sam, when he left hospital. It was hard work for a double crew. It would be very hard work single handed. There was no time to lose.

It was barely light when he let go, and headed north. There would be no time for enjoying the countryside. No chance to chat. He would rise to the challenge. He would not let Sam down, and nor would the Phoenix. The engine started at the first attempt. The steady thump, thump, thump was like music to his ears.

***

Jack was looking forward to seeing Sam. He had enjoyed the responsibility of working Phoenix single handed, but he missed the companionship. Sharing breakfast, and chatting into the late evening, he missed the most. He was too busy in the day to think of much. There were sections of the canal free of locks where he could relax to some degree, and enjoy the countryside. But these were few and far between. At these times his mind would think of many things. He would think of Sam of course. But most of the time his mind was in Newton Magna with his family and friends.

He would also think about the world in which he now lived. Here was a world where nothing was wasted. A world where partnerships worked, and families were happy and content. The work was hard, but nobody shirked or complained. Handouts were what you got at meal times, as the boat never stopped moving. There was no stopping for lunch, time was money. The pay was poor, but needs were simple. Children that had been confined to the cabin in the day were happy to play tag, or sometimes play simple games in the hold when the boats were empty. Jack had even seen children playing on a makeshift swing that had been rigged up in one empty vessel.

The roads were relatively quiet, and most goods were transported safely by rail or water. How short sighted the politicians of the latter years, who let concrete and tarmac scars deface this beautiful land of ours, whilst railways and canals, which had long ago blended in, were left to fester and decay.

THIRTY FOUR

No Leg To Stand On

The doctor had agreed to Sam's discharge provided that there was someone to escort him. As Jack was not able to come to the hospital, Sam had managed to persuade a delivery man to drop him off at the local train station. With the aid of a porter Sam struggled into a carriage, and settled himself down as best he could. Just how he was going to get from Braunston Station to the canal was a problem he had not yet resolved. And of course, the rendezvous with Jack had been arranged via third, fourth, and even fifth parties, so there was no guarantee that Jack would even be there to meet him.

As the train came to a halt Sam lifted himself from his seat, hobbled to the door, and dropped the window. As he reached for the handle he spotted Jack at the end of the platform.

"You must be joking, you don't expect me to travel in

that do you?" Sam said, as Jack approached.

"Well I'm not going to carry you, so what other choice do we have?"

"Good point."

"Come on then, park your bum."

With Jack's assistance, Sam lowered himself into the wheelbarrow. His left leg hung over the battered front edge, whilst his plastered right leg pointed the way.

"You be careful young Jack, one break's quite enough."

Jack took a deep breath, and lifted his nervous load. But Sam needn't have worried, Jack had a safe pair of hands. They were back at the Phoenix in no time. Getting onto the boat was another matter.

Jack couldn't help himself; he just had to laugh.

"Yes, very funny. Now help me get on this bloody boat," Sam said. He was obviously becoming frustrated by his lack of mobility. Before leaving hospital Sam had done his best to make himself look decent. He had cut his trousers up the seam, in order to make them fit over the plaster on his right leg, and had used several pieces of stout cord to hold the material together.

But it would be some weeks before Sam would be back to normal. No steering for Jack. He would have to work all the locks. He would certainly be fit by the time that Sam's plaster was removed.

Jack helped Sam climb aboard. That was the easy part. With his leg plastered from thigh to ankle, negotiating the cabin step was far more difficult.

"I'll manage Jack, you just stand there laughing."

But the problem was that he didn't manage. The metal

loop on the bottom of his foot slipped on the hatch step, and he shot into the cabin like a rat down a drain pipe. Jack lost all control, and nearly fell into the cut. He was still laughing as they shared a pot of tea. But no further harm had been done, and even Sam saw the funny side of the incident.

"Better wrap some cloth round that loop Sam. Don't want you taking a look."

It would be a wise precaution. If Sam was to slip off the boat whilst Jack was some distance away, he would find it extremely difficult to save himself.

THIRTY FIVE

What's Up Doc?

Over the following weeks, despite Sam's lack of movement, Jack and Sam became a very accomplished crew. Jack's muscles developed, and hardened. He could now wind up the paddles very quickly, and the lock gates were no longer a problem.

It was during this time that Jack asked Sam a question one evening, as they enjoyed a bite to eat.

"Do you have any books Sam?"

"Not a lot of point."

"You mean you don't have time to read them?"

Sam sucked hard on his pipe. "Never had no need," he said after a while. It was obvious that he was uncomfortable with the topic, and Jack decided to change the subject.

As Jack later thought about his conversation with Sam, he realized that the boat children had little time for schooling. They were always on the move. And if each generation had worked the boats, then just how much education could they have received. He decided not to raise the subject again. However, another thought did enter his head.

***

It was good to get the plaster off, but the look on the doctor's face told Sam that all was not as it should be.

"Go on then Doc. What's the problem?"

"Well, it's mended Mister Forbes, but it's not quite perfect."

"Oh yes, and what do you mean by that?"

"It's not as straight as we'd hoped it would be, and the muscle's a bit twisted."

"But that'll get better with use, won't it?"

"Yes, I'm sure it will. But take it steady to start with. The leg will still feel a bit weak."

Sam couldn't disguise just how he felt, when Jack joined him.

"Not too good Jack. Leg's not going to be as good as it was."

"I'm sure you'll be all right Sam. I'll do everything you can't until it gets stronger."

"I know you will, you're a good lad Jack."

***

Jack sat on the roof of the cabin, his legs dangling over the side. He was careful not to damage the paintwork. Sam was justifiably proud of the Phoenix, and Jack had no intention of upsetting the good relationship they had. He couldn't help but think how nice it would have been, had he been this close to his own father.

The setting sun worked its magic in what was otherwise a rather drab area. The brasses on the chimneys sent a thousand golden jewels of light dancing across the water, which was already dappled where the sun's rays could penetrate the lush foliage on the western bank. All about him, the boat people were busy, polishing, scrubbing, and cleaning. Children were playing games. They appeared happy, their lives were simple, but they were content. The men and women were uneducated, but skilled in their work. They had family values, and respect for one another. Parents educated their offspring in the ways of the boat people. They had no books, but they spoke to each other.

Jack marvelled at the dexterity of one man splicing a rope. Sam sat puffing on his pipe; his day's work done. Jack decided that, if he was to remain in this age, he too would be content. The work was hard but satisfying, the people a close knit community.

The evening was concluded, like so many others, with a drink in the nearby public house. That night Jack slipped into a deep sleep within moments of closing his eyes. He had decided that, if he was to be a boatman, he would be one of the best. He would learn all he could from Sam, and from anyone who was willing to teach him. It was as though the old Jack had been reborn. Of course he thought about his family, he thought about them a lot. He tried to soften the sharp edges of the pain by telling himself there was nothing he could do. It wasn't like a normal separation, where a search can bring a positive result. No search could span the years.

And as Jack lay awake in the early hours of the following morning, the sounds of steam locomotives were somehow comforting. They were living creatures that breathed smoke and steam. You could tell when they were working hard, or coasting easily. Or when they were in a hurry, or marking time. It came to him, just how lucky he was. Not for him the illustrated history books. Here was a world that his contemporaries would never know. Yet another thought also entered his head. In this time, he knew so much of the future. Should he tell Sam and the others what was to be? Would he have wanted to know his future? No, better to live each day to the full, and celebrate life itself. For within a decade, this wonderful Country would once again be plunged into conflict, and young lives would be so tragically snatched away.

***

The days passed quickly, and the weeks slipped by. The skin on Jack's hands hardened, his arms grew in strength, and he felt alive. Through the fatigue, and hard reality of life on the cut, a deep satisfaction helped him sleep soundly at night. There were even moments, though they were few and far between, when he forgot that he did not belong in this time.

THIRTY SIX

Good News

"Have you seen the headlines?" Carol Fletcher asked, the moment that her husband stepped through the front door.

"Well no, I haven't had the chance love."

"Silly me, of course you haven't. I'll put the kettle on."

"Haven't you forgotten something?" Paul said, as he put down his briefcase, and slipped off his shoes.

"Sorry dear, mind on other things." Carol returned to the hall and gave Paul a kiss.

"Paper's on the table."

Paul Fletcher picked up the newspaper, and smiled. He began reading. 'Corruption in Local Council? It is alleged that corrupt practise in the Wayborough Council has led to the arrests of Councillor Geoffrey Booth and businessman Richard Graham.'

It continued. 'Plans to build a number of Executive

Houses in Newton Magna have now been shelved. Local Police Officer Toby Morton has been commended for his diligence and hard work concerning these investigations.'

"You look happy dear, had a good day?" Carol said as she brought in the tea.

"Very good indeed, in fact couldn't be better in the circumstances."

THIRTY SEVEN

New Friends

It was one evening as Jack sat reading that another chapter started in his life.

"What's it about, mister?" A small girl asked. Jack hadn't heard her approach

"It's called The Time Machine, by H.G. WELLS."

"What's a time machine?"

"It's something that allows you to travel through time."

"But you can't really do that can you?"

Jack smiled. "It's just a story, a very good one. Would you like me to read to you?"

"Yes please mister, and could Alfie and Charlie come as well?"

"Are they your brothers?"

"Yes."

"And what's your name?"

"Rose, the same as me mam."

"Well ask your mam if it's all right."

Rose hurried off to fetch her brothers. In no time at all the three had become ten or more, as the children from various boats gathered round to hear the story. Mothers were glad of the chance to clean up, with the children safely out of the way. They knew that no harm would come to them whilst they were with Jack. News had already spread about him saving the little boy from the water.

From that day on, Jack regularly read to the children, whenever an opportunity arose.

***

Sam was curious. He had watched Jack reading to the children on a number of occasions, and would have liked to have joined the group. He was a proud man, and would not ask for help. But the book fascinated him.

Sam was carefully turning the pages when Jack returned to the boat one evening.

"Want to read it Sam?" Jack blurted out, before he had thought about his words.

"Er, no but thank you Jack, I was just looking."

Jack thought very carefully before he spoke again.

"Sam, I've noticed that the boat children don't get much education. They don't get the opportunity."

"They can't really, it's not that they don't want to learn."

"I know, but if the boats have been worked by the same families over the generations, there has been little chance for anyone to learn."

"Well yes, I suppose you're right."

Jack bit his lip and decided he would be more direct. He didn't want to hurt Sam's feelings, but he wanted to give him an opportunity, one that Sam had never had.

"Sam, you're an expert with the boat, no one can deny that."

Sam smiled, but said nothing.

"And you can work wonders with the engine, and.............."

"No Jack, I can't read nor write. Is that what you wanted to know?"

"Well yes it was."

"Never had the need really." Sam said, relighting his pipe.

"Would you like me to teach you Sam? That's if you don't mind"

"I'd like that Jack, I'd like that very much. Then I could write to Ruth."

Jack thought about his world, a world of mobile phones, and text messaging. Here just a lifetime previously, phones were a rarity. And the thought of the technology that he knew was in the imagination of the few.

It would be no good using the book he had. He would have to find something far more straightforward. The next time he had the chance, he would get a suitable book. In the meantime he would start with the basics.

Each day thereafter followed the same pattern. When all work was done, and the meal eaten, Jack would spend some time teaching Sam. It was an unusual situation, a teenager teaching a middle aged man. But both seemed comfortable with the arrangement. Jack in particular, welcomed the chance to repay Sam for his kindness. After all he was learning a lot from Sam, a master in the school of life.

THIRTY EIGHT

Vultures

It had been some time since Toby Morton had allowed himself time to relax. That first pint was like nectar.

"I'll never understand the way some people think," Joe Richards suddenly said, as he selected another glass, held it up to the light, and then polished it with his cloth.

"What don't you understand?"

"Well, it's the same when an accident happens; or a major disaster."

Toby waited for the next line, but Joe was busying himself with yet another glass. In the end he had to speak.

"Are you going to actually tell me what you're thinking, or just give me the odd cryptic clue?"

"Sorry Toby, what was I saying?"

"You were talking about people, accidents, and major disasters."

"Well you know what I mean. It's the way that some

people thrive on other people's misery."

"You mean like people who watch fires, and stop at the scene of accidents; not to help, but just to look?"

"Yes, that sort of thing."

"Can't say as I've given it much thought."

"Well, ever since the television coverage about the two boys, my takings have been up. It looks like we'll be able to manage after all. Reckon I'll submit them papers for the restaurant idea that Kath has."

Toby turned on his stool. Joe was right; the bar was pretty full.

It was indeed rare to see Toby in the Bull's Head. He had pushed himself very hard. He had long before decided that, if he couldn't find the boys, or any clues as to their whereabouts, it wouldn't be for the lack of trying. He would leave no stone unturned. And when Paul Fletcher had told him about the suspected corruption in the Council, he had thrown himself headlong into that investigation as well. It had meant working long hours, and getting very little sleep, but sleep had been the last thing on his mind. The adrenalin had been pumping through his body, his new leaner body. His regular visits to the Bull's Head had been put on hold. Meals were light snacks, taken when he could afford a few moments. Even his uniform had had to be exchanged for a smaller size.

THIRTY NINE

Genesis

It was quite the largest gathering in the village since the start of the searches for the boys. But this gathering involved the whole village in a way that no one had expected.

Paul Fletcher was to be the main speaker, with John Pollard assisting. John was not a public speaker by any stretch of the imagination, but if he was comfortable with his audience, and his subject, he would, ''ave a go.' Ray Bridges had helped set up the chairs and tables in the old Village Hall, and Cathy Bridges and Carol Fletcher had organised refreshments.

When everyone had taken their seats Paul Fletcher stood up to speak.

"Good evening ladies and gentlemen, thank you for coming. Just to let you know what to expect, I'll quickly run through what we intend to do this evening. Firstly I'll outline the proposals, and the background behind them.

Then John will say a few words."

"Get him started, you'll never shut him up," someone shouted from the back of the room.

Paul Fletcher smiled, waited until the audience had settled once again, and continued. "Then we will show you a detailed plan and model for you to inspect. Carol and Cathy will serve refreshments; after which we'll have an open forum to discuss matters. I would ask you to please keep your questions until the time of this forum. Thank you."

Once again there was a certain amount of conversation within the crowd. Paul Fletcher gave the audience a few moments, waiting for the hall to once again become quiet.

"Many of you will have been following the reports in the papers, concerning certain goings on in the local council. Well let me tell you that the proposals to build executive style houses on Mr Pollard's land have been scrapped. Mr Pollard however, was willing to consider other proposals for the land, and has provisionally accepted my offer. In a moment I will show you what I propose."

Paul Fletcher sat down, and John Pollard rose to his feet. He explained his reason for selling part of his land, and said that he was more than pleased to deal with Mr Fletcher.

John Pollard then said something that Paul Fletcher was not expecting. "You all know me. I was born in this village. My father was born here, as was his father. We've worked the farm, and taken the rough with the smooth. There's many people here tonight who weren't born in the village. That's no fault of theirs. I say it's about time we stopped this us and them, and joined forces for the good of Newton Magna."

There was a moments silence, and then the whole audience applauded. John Pollard turned to Paul Fletcher and said, "Right now it's your turn."

"Thank you John."

Between them they moved their table to one side, and opened the curtains immediately behind. There, laid out on a number of tables that had been pulled together, was a scale model of Paul's vision.

As the crowd gathered round, Joe Richards was the first to speak.

"Well blow me, it's a marina."

Indeed it was. The model showed an area of John Pollard's land that abutted the canal, a short distance from the bottom lock. There were model narrow boats moored, a boat services and hire base, and various other buildings. These included what looked like small cottages, slightly higher up, but overlooking the marina. It was some time before the audience returned to their seats. Paul Fletcher had asked everyone to be patient, he would answer their questions shortly.

"Thank you ladies and gentlemen, your questions please."

Although there were many, no one seemed opposed to the plan. It would be a joint enterprise between Paul Fletcher Associates, the Local Council, and The Canal and River Trust. The boat hire base, that was presently situated a short distance from the village would relocate, and there would be employment opportunities created. In addition, the cottages would be jointly owned by the Council, and the first time buyers, thus keeping the price down for local people.

***

It was a happy Paul Fletcher that saw the last person away, before helping to clear up.

"Think we'll have a little celebration at the pub, if that's all right with you Mr Fletcher?" Joe Richards said, as the small group left the caretaker to lock up.

"They say every cloud has a silver lining," Ray Bridges said, as they walked towards the Bull's Head. "I know that our cloud has been pretty dark, but it looks like the future of the village will be secured," he added.

"It'll be something to tell the boys when they get back," Paul Fletcher said. He was determined to remain positive at all times. At least the project would keep them all occupied.

FORTY

The Circle Turns

"They've got trouble with that embankment again Jack. No doubt the heavy rain has had an effect. Going to fix it properly this time though with concrete and stuff."

"Does that mean we'll be using the old canal up through Newton Magna again?" Jack asked.

"Yes, not a lot of choice really. At least if we use it now and again they'll have to keep it open. Mind you, if they fix the cut proper, they might not think it necessary like."

"Don't worry Sam, they'll keep it open."

"Oh yes, got a crystal ball then have you Jack?"

"No, just a feeling Sam, just a feeling."

It had been six months since they had met at the locks. It would be strange to work through them again now, with Jack as a crew mate, and not an inquisitive schoolboy.

The water was low, and a lot of silt restricted the channel to the centre of the canal. Several times Jack felt the mud beneath the boat, as she slid along, reliable engine thumping away.

Being used to well-maintained locks on the 'Main Line', it came as a shock to Jack when he came to the first lock on the old canal. There was no paint on the balance beams; it had long ago flaked and peeled. The gates leaked badly, and weeds grew from the topmost planks, that stood above the water. Paddle winding mechanisms were dry and devoid of grease. All things that he had taken no notice of six months back. But that was understandable as he had been in shock at that time. The locks were hard work, but they still functioned. Jack found it heart–breaking to see the canal in such a neglected and forlorn condition.

FORTY ONE

A Debt Repaid

As Jack lay in his bed that night, staring into the darkness, his mind jumped from one event to another. And from nineteen thirty to home and back again. It was the sound of the train in the distance that brought other memories flooding back. Jack sat up and lit the lamp. Then he rummaged through his clothes – it just had to be there somewhere. Jack felt the edge of the small piece of cardboard and quickly pulled it out. It was somewhat tatty; but it had definitely once been a railway ticket. With it was a fragment of paper.

Jack dressed quickly, and quietly so as to not wake Sam. He pressed the two items into his jacket pocket, and opened the door as quietly as he could. He didn't risk sliding the hatch forward, he knew the noise that it could make at times. He crawled out on all fours, gently closed the door behind him, and stepped from the boat. Even this he did carefully so that no rocking movement could be felt. He lifted old Betsy from the storage position, and set off down the towpath.

It was a clear, moonlit night, and Jack was able to safely negotiate the many hazards on the approach to the bridge. Once on the road he made good progress. It was a good distance, but Jack was young and fit. There before him was the old farm. Jack smiled a warm smile as he kept the promise he'd made so long ago. He was back at the boat, and asleep, in no time. Sam didn't even know that he'd been away.

FORTY TWO

Deja vu

Jack had noticed a difference in Sam that morning. He could tell that he had something to say. It was just a matter of waiting patiently.

Jack had a strange feeling that he couldn't explain as they headed towards his home village. Even the weather was changing. Where a short while previously, the sun had shone in a clear blue sky, clouds were gathering fast, and the temperature had dropped.

It was mid-afternoon as they approached Newton Magna bottom lock. By now the sun had disappeared, and the light was an eerie mixture of orange and grey. Jack had only ever seen it like this on one previous occasion.

Sam suddenly reached inside the hatch to get his jacket. It looked as if Jack's patience was about to pay off.

"I know that you've always admired my leather belt Jack, so I've got a little surprise for you."

He took a package from his jacket pocket, and handed it to Jack.

"Thank you Sam."

It had been a long time since Jack had received a present. He unfolded the top of the brown paper package, and his eyes lit up as he looked inside. There, neatly rolled, was a brown leather belt, complete with highly polished brass buckle. Jack left the belt in its wrapping.

"I'll try it on later," he said. "My hands are filthy. I don't want to ruin it. Thank you again."

"I hope the belt will remind you of the time we've spent together. I'm going to miss you Jack."

"What do you mean?"

Sam was finding it difficult, but he had practised the words many times in his head.

"It's time I left the cut Jack. The life doesn't suit my old leg, too much abuse. Besides, I've asked Ruth to marry me and she's accepted. I can help her on the farm.

"But how did you manage that? We've not seen her for some time, and I've not helped you with any letter."

"Don't need no schooling to use the telephone Jack. Once they showed me how, I had a go. Clever things them telephones. Like being with someone, but with your eyes shut."

"So when did you use a telephone?"

"When I was went back to the hospital, to get the plaster off me busted leg."

"You crafty old devil."

Sam smiled the biggest smile.

"But won't you miss the boats Sam?"

"I dare say that I will, but we won't be that far from the cut, will we?"

Jack pushed the bag into his jacket pocket, and set off to prepare the lock. It was strange to think, that the last time that he had seen this particular lock was in his own time.

Jack swung open the lock gates, and sat resting on the balance beam waiting for the familiar sound of the old diesel engine. But the sound never came. Jack looked down, and saw the fresh black and white paint that he knew so well. But his obvious delight at returning to his own time was tinged with sadness as he looked along the canal. Sam and the Phoenix had become just memories.

FORTY THREE

Present Day

Jack looked at his clothes. He had forgotten what it was like to wear jeans and trainers. Clothes were one thing, his hands and arms were another. His hands were rough and calloused, his forearms bronzed and muscular. It was good to have his wristwatch again, although he could see that it had stopped. The battery must have run down whilst he was away. Jack thrust his hands into his pockets. The belt he had stolen from Bussey's shop was still there. Whatever else he was planning, it would have to wait.

As he moved away from the canal he felt as though part of him had died. Never again would it be just somewhere to while away his time. As he stood thinking he could just make out the sound of machinery not too far away. He would discover its purpose sometime later.

Jack realized that, having been away from the village for so long, the second hand shop might not now be there.

***

He need not have worried.

"I'm sorry Mr Bussey," Jack blurted out as he pushed the leather belt into the shopkeepers hand. Bartholomew Bussey just smiled an even broader smile than usual.

"You knew that I would come back, didn't you?" Jack said, as he started to regain his breath.

"Oh yes," said the shopkeeper. "It was only a matter of time."

"But I've done so many bad things, Mr B. I wish that I could alter the past."

"No one can do that Jack, they can only shape the future."

"But how can you do that?"

"By doing the right things today, and each and every day. You see, one day Jack, even this day will be in the past. The only way to change it is to do it now."

Jack thought he understood. He thanked Mr Bussey for his kindness and turned as if to leave.

"Haven't you forgotten something young man?"

"I don't think so," Jack replied.

"The belt, you had better take it with you."

"But it's not mine."

"Oh I think that you will find it is. Have a better look."

Jack took the belt and uncurled it. On the inside, written in black ink, was the wording.......

TO MY FRIEND JACK,
WITH THANKS SAM FORBES.

Jack slipped the belt into his pocket, smiled, and hurried from the shop. He didn't want anyone to see the tears in his eyes.

He had only gone about ten yards when he spun around and returned to the doorway. The shopkeeper was waiting.

"Do you know what happened to my friend Rob, while I've been away?" Jack said.

"I wondered when you would ask about young Rob. Unfortunately he won't be returning to the village for a while, if at all. Not everyone takes advantage of a second chance."

Jack thought of asking more questions, but decided to leave it for now. He thanked Mr Bussey once more, and headed for home. Just what story he was going to tell, after being away for six months, he hadn't yet worked out.

FORTY FOUR

All Change

As Jack approached the house, he couldn't help noticing a few changes. The garden was neat and tidy, the grass closely cropped, and there was a lovely display of flowers. The car in the driveway was also different. The Five Series BMW. had gone. In its place was a modest estate car. He could tell that it was his father's car though, the personalised number plate had been retained. It had been an anniversary present between his parents a couple of years previously. But why change the car, thought Jack, the Five was practically new?

Jack turned his key in the lock and slowly opened the front door.

"Mum, Dad, I'm back."

Carol and Paul Fletcher appeared in the kitchen doorway. For a moment there was the silence of disbelief. Then Carol Fletcher rushed forward.

"Jack," was all she could manage to say before her arms were round him, and she was sobbing on his shoulder. Paul Fletcher wrapped his arms around them both. It was Jack that spoke first.

"What happened to the car?"

"I thought it would be better for when we go fishing."

"But you never have time to take me anywhere?"

"I will have in the future. It's time we saw more of each other. After all, you only get one go at this life thing."

It was so unreal to be talking like this, but where do you start when your son has been missing for six months.

"We'd better let P.C. Withers know that you're back, safe and well," Carol Fletcher said, when she finally stopped hugging her son.

"Who's P.C. Withers?" Jack asked.

"Oh, of course you wouldn't know would you? P.C. Withers has replaced Toby Morton as the village policeman."

"Then what's happened to Toby Morton?"

"He's now Sergeant Morton, in charge of the police station at Market Clayton."

"You look well Jack," his mother said, as she wiped away her tears Wherever you've been, it must have suited you."

"Let's put it this way, it did me good."

"You can tell us all about your adventures, once you've settled in," his mother said.

I don't think so, Jack thought.

"No pressure though," Paul Fletcher said. "We're not going to interrogate you. We're just so glad to have you safely home."

"You say it's done you good Jack; it's done us good too," his father added. "We've made a few decisions whilst you've been missing."

Paul Fletcher outlined his plans for the future, for the future of the family, and the village. Jack had also made plans, but they could wait until later. It was Paul Fletcher's next statement that surprised Jack the most.

"And I thought that we could have a holiday on the canals this year. A real family holiday. You can even have a go at steering the boat, something not too big though. Do you think that you'd enjoy that Jack? I'm sure you'd soon get the hang of it."

***

Jack didn't get much sleep that night. In fact he didn't get any sleep at all. It was fortunate that the next day was Saturday, and not a school day.

***

It was late the next afternoon when Mrs Rodgers called round to see Jack's mum.

"You know Carol," she said, "Somebody drained part of the canal last night, you ought to see the mess in the mud. Whoever it was must have been pretty desperate to find something."

Jack said nothing.

"That's not the only strange thing," Carol Fletcher replied.

"When old Mr Riley fetched his milk in this morning, he found more than a pint of semi–skimmed. Someone had returned his medals."

Jack munched on his sandwich, and smiled.